STORMBOUND

J. C. McKenzie

The wind sliced through his fur and chafed at his hide. His eyes felt as though they blistered. A dark cabin looming in the field of white. Finally. The Jones' cabin.

He charged up the steps to the front entrance, finally stopping where the overhang protected the patio from the snow.

Brenna swung her leg over his shoulders and dismounted. Sort of. More like she fell off. She winced and sucked back air. He leaned forward, trying to offer her help, but she scooted out of his reach.

"I'm fine," she hissed.

Obviously.

In the protected area of the main entrance, Brenna pulled down her face guard again and pursed her lips. Darkness shrouded her fine features, but a trail of dried blood from her forehead and mouth indicated she'd hit her head. He hadn't paused to assess her injuries before taking her to the cabin. His heart beat heavy in his chest. If that twit hadn't lost her gloves...If he hadn't gone for a run...

She sniffed the air around them and her whole body stiffened. Her gaze turned hard. "Eric Buchanan."

Cormorant Run
"CORMORANT RUN by J.C. McKenzie is an amazing dystopic science fiction read that will have you mesmerized from the first word to the last."
~ Fresh Fiction

The Night House
"From the very first page till the very end I was hooked on this book and read it in less than one day...it had everything you could want from a story romance, secrets, lies, suspense, surprises and more."
~ Paranormal Romance Guild

Shift Happens
"SHIFT HAPPENS has excitement, intrigue and lots of danger. I love the whole cast of characters and how they played a part in the story" ~ Fresh Fiction

Beast Coast
"I loved this book as much as the first. There are secrets, surprises, and all manner of supernaturals."
~ Paranormal Romance Guild

Carpe Demon
"The story keeps the adrenaline pumping and spine tingling tension building throughout the story with well written scenes full of vivid details that capture the imagination and make it easy for the reader to become engrossed..." ~ Literary Addicts Book Community

Shift Work
"It's a terrific series and if you like supernatural reads, with a side of romance, the sort with solid and intense plots, gripping and very real dangers, hard choices, supernatural people some of whom can be selfish, cruel and bloodthirsty...You'll be hooked."
~ Jeannie Zelos Book Reviews

Beast of All
"This time out, J. C. McKenzie has outdone herself with high-velocity action, soul deep emotions and one of those finishes that you want to replay over and over!"
~ Tome Tender

Dangerous Dreams
"This new world promises to be an adventurous one full of snark, passion, thrills, romance, danger and wonderful characters and I can't wait to read the next one." ~ Stormy Vixen Reviews

Dangerous Liaisons
"Loved this story and loved Raf and strong, stubborn Lara and I can't overlook Lara's dragon who brought humor to this story." ~ Paranormal Romance Guild

The Good Griffin
"THE GOOD GRIFFIN is as addictive as a double shot of espresso, only without any of the withdrawal symptoms." ~ N. N. Light

COPYRIGHT INFORMATION

Contact Information: jcmckenzie@jcmckenzie.ca

Cover Art: BRoseDesignz

Publishing History:

First JCM Publications Edition, 2020

ISBN: 978-1-990143-05-2 (print)

ISBN: 978-1-990143-06-9 (ebook)

To all the lovers who believe in second chances.

"Sometimes you don't have the words to express your feelings."

— *NECCO, CREATOR OF SWEETHEARTS*

CHAPTER 1

What was Brenna thinking? Why had she insisted on travelling to her parents' remote cabin to spend Valentine's Day weekend by herself? She could've curled up with books in her own apartment, but nooooo...the call of the wild, a crackling log fireplace, and the stillness the city couldn't offer beckoned like a late-night lover. Brenna might be a null wolf—unable to transform into her animal form and considered the lowest of the low in werewolf hierarchy—but she still craved nature and the solace found in the winter forest.

The old rust bucket truck chortled along the snow-packed road. The engine's familiar rumble drowned out the oldies rocking out from the ancient AM/FM radio. This far from the city and without the ability to connect her phone, the radio station was her only option to fill the silence and she loved it. Every song brought back a fond childhood memory, most of which involved her singing along to songs with her family in this very truck.

I loved those trips, Maisie said before launching into her own interpretation of a crooning ballad. Brenna couldn't shift into a wolf, but she still had one in her head. Kids in her pack and the neighbouring ones used to call her double cursed. Sometimes, like right now, she agreed. Maisie couldn't hit a note if her life depended on it.

Brenna reached for another candy heart, a childish family tradition, but probably as romantic as her weekend would get. If only—

The old pickup truck swerved, fishtailing on the snow-packed road. Ice. Her heart convulsed as she clutched the steering wheel and tried to regain control.

Now you've done it, Maisie whispered in her head.

The truck hit a snow drift. The engine revved, and the truck launched into the air. Sudden weightlessness consumed her. Time slowed. As if by sheer brain power alone, the vehicle hovered midflight on its path toward a massive snowbank and inevitable impact. Instead of any survival instincts, she used the precious time to berate herself. Why'd she take her eyes off the road to grab a candy heart? Stupid, stupid, stupid. This little treat would literally be the death of her.

There're better ways to go, Maisie griped.

Brenna's heartbeat thudded in her ears. Sweat broke out and prickled her skin. Time sped up. No longer stuck on pause, the truck continued to barrel toward the snowbank. Before impact, she released the steering wheel and covered her head with her arms.

Images flashed through her memory—hot summer road trips with her girlfriends, Christmas with her parents, her brother's cheeky grin as he pulled her pigtails, and her first true kiss from a boy with sandy brown hair and piercing green eyes.

The truck struck the hard-packed, unforgiving snowbank. The impact jarred the vehicle, crunching metal.

Brenna whipped forward. Her seatbelt snagged and dug into her chest, her forehead smacking her arms before bashing into the steering wheel. Pain erupted in her skull. Her head snapped back and everything went black.

Brenna's head pounded as her vision cleared. Maisie howling in her mind didn't make things better, either. Blood trickled from her forehead and mouth. Her tongue ached from when she'd bitten down, and her gums hurt as if her teeth still rattled. She'd hit her head pretty hard. Hopefully, she didn't damage anything too much.

The smell of coffee permeated the truck. Her travel mug lay open on the seat beside her, and the remains of glorious caffeine trickled down the inside of the windshield and onto the dash. The heart-shaped candies lay scattered across the cab.

The wind outside muffled any potential sound except the buzzing of her head. Snow covered the cracked windshield. The rear passenger window had shattered, spraying chunks of glass over her bags. The heat had long since leeched out, and the air whistled through the glass and around the truck.

We're screwed, Maisie said. Helpful as always.

Looking through the windshield provided little information. Snow, snow and more snow.

So much snow, it blanketed her vision to the outside world. She didn't dare open her door or window. As chilled as her bones were now, outside would be colder. She didn't have the advantage of a wolf form to keep her warm if she got trapped in the snow. No increased strength. No accelerated healing. Only a heightened sense of smell and an eccentric voice in her head.

I resent that, Maisie grumbled.

Brenna ignored her wolf and wiggled her toes. Yup, still working. Fingers? Fine. Body? Needed a long soak in a bathtub, but everything seemed okay. She reached over and plucked a candy heart from the passenger seat. It read, CHILL OUT. Fitting. She popped the sweet candy in her mouth and paused to let the flavour coat her tongue as her racing heart slowed down. She needed to focus. Evaluate. She might not be a super strong or super aggressive werewolf, but she had a brain.

With shaking hands, she leaned forward and turned the key to the ignition. The engine chugged before choking out. She tried again. Nothing.

"Come on!" she pleaded.

Still nothing.

She tried again.

"Come on, baby." The engine sputtered, but quickly died.

Old Blue, her beloved truck, was dead. Well, technically, it was her father's truck. She pulled her phone from her jacket pocket and touched the screen. No service. Of course not. Poor cell reception in the mountains wasn't a surprise, but why couldn't she catch a break? Encased in a snow-tomb wasn't how she wanted to go out.

What the hell would she do?

No one came up here. Especially not in a blizzard. She was probably the only fool within a fifty-kilometer radius. If she stayed in the truck, she risked getting buried under snow and with the window broken, the cab of the truck only offered a reprieve from the skin cutting wind and damp snow as an advantage.

She couldn't stay.

But should she leave? With night falling, walking through deep snow in a winter storm surrounded by a forest with wolves might prove fatal. Real wolves wouldn't care about the voice in her head.

Damned if she did, damned if she didn't.

Brenna turned to haul the emergency kit from the backseat. The red and black canvas material of the bag made it easy to spot, but not so easy to grab. Pain lanced across her body. Her sore chest complained, and her knees ached. The sudden movement made her vision swim, and the dull throb behind her eyes intensified.

Brenna reached to unclip her seatbelt. The button jammed.

"Crap!" She yanked on the buckle, but it remained cemented in. Argh! If only she had werewolf super strength.

Maisie huffed.

With gritted teeth, she turned and tried to grab the kit again. She stretched her arm out, fumbling with her fingers to grip the strap.

A little farther!

She needed that pack. With a sucked in breath, she pushed against the strap as it dug into the bruised flesh between her breasts and thrust her hand out. Pain streaked down her limbs and exploded in her back. She grabbed the strap and hauled the bag from the back-seat. A deep sigh escaped her lungs. Success. She panted and waited for the pain to ebb.

With a blanket, her jacket, toque, and gloves, she'd survive the night and try her luck in the morning. With the Buchanan's as the nearest cabin other than her parents', she doubted a rescue would happen. Besides...

She'd rather the snow's company than the Buchanan's son.

Brenna unzipped the red and black bag to retrieve the large hunting knife. With a quick swipe of the sharp blade, she freed herself from the seatbelt.

Now what?

Brenna reached forward and pulled her keys from the ignition. She nestled into her jacket and hunkered down for a long, lonely and cold night. Maybe a patrol would brave the elements, and she'd be saved by the man of her dreams.

Brenna snorted.

That would never happen. She had the worst luck with men.

CHAPTER 2

E ric cursed his family and their not-so-subtle attempts to set him up. Again. Not only was Heather Dufaine a shallow airhead with the personality of puff cereal, but snowmobiling as a storm rolled in had to be the dumbest idea ever. He didn't care if her father was the alpha of an allied pack, this match would never happen.

The rising sun cast the hills and valleys of snow in sporadic shadows. Night fell fast in the B.C. Rockies, but it left the same way. His paws sunk into the deep snow as he charged up another bank. He slowed as the wind blew another gust of snow across his path, and his visibility fell from ten percent to zero. With his dense winter coat and frost-bite resistant paws, he'd survive this outing, but if he didn't run off some of this anger, no one else would when he returned to the crowded cabin.

Heather had insisted on going out last night, and his family encouraged him to indulge her. As if she were some petulant child threatening a tantrum. Heck, one look at her pouty face confirmed his guess wasn't far off.

Why on earth his parents wanted her as a daughter-in-law had stumped him for all of two seconds. Her "daddy" and his father were judges and both alphas of their respective packs. Though they already had an alliance, the idea of a marriage between their two prominent families would unify the two packs and solidify their position as the area's powerhouse.

It didn't matter to anyone that they weren't true mates. Those were so rare to find these days.

Luckily, he'd convinced Heather a half-hour into snowmobiling the conditions were too dangerous, and he'd returned her in one piece to his family's cabin with the mistaken belief he cared for her.

He certainly didn't wish her harm. It wasn't her fault she'd been raised entitled and brainwashed into believing happiness only fit in a certain box.

Happiness.

What would he know about that?

The only time he found true happiness in the arms of a woman was a long time ago, and the moment fleeting at best. He'd had his true mate in his hands, but instead of welcoming the moment, instead of submitting to the call, he freaked out and hurt her irreparably. She rejected him for it.

That short moment in time and his split-second decision impacted the rest of his life. Sometimes he questioned whether it even happened.

Now, he found enjoyment in the wilderness, with the sharp scent of pine and the cold bite of the air. Eric tucked his head and charged over another ridge. The frozen air sliced over him, and he sped up the next bank.

Heather had lost her favorite pink mittens. When he'd first spotted the delicate things, he'd suggested she wear hardier gloves to protect her sensitive skin. Werewolf or not, the human form was vulnerable, and the wind up here was unforgivingly cold. Heather had opted to follow his advice, but instead of leaving her own mittens at the cabin, she tucked them in her back pocket. When he'd finally herded her to the cabin, she discovered they'd fallen out.

She cried.

Over pink mittens.

The goddamn daughter of the Sapphire Wolf Pack sniffled over winter attire.

If he hadn't already known, that moment would've confirmed no future existed between them. Even if his father hadn't gloated about Eric's "formidable tracking skills," he still would've leapt at the chance to retrieve the stupid mittens. Anything to escape the small cabin and get away from his meddling parents. He left first thing in the morning with the storm still raging.

Now, he raced around as the snowstorm really set

in, with no real intent to find any pink accessories, and enjoyed a few moments of freedom without the incessant nagging of his mom, or bragging of his father. As the conditions worsened, however, he cursed his own stupidity along with his parents.

He shouldn't have taken the route passing the Jones' cabin. Of course, Brenna wouldn't be there. Although her parents and brother visited the vacation cabin often, Brenna rarely returned since the summer after high school graduation.

Brenna Jones.

Mate, Brutus whined.

He shook his head. *Not anymore.*

An image of light elfin eyes framed with white hair flashed across his mind.

Ten years later and he still thought about her. As a null wolf from a small pack, Brenna had to deal with a lot of crap growing up, and he'd added to it. All through school, he'd liked her, but he also resented her for it. As the heir to the Topaz Mountain Pack, he shouldn't have been drawn to a weak null. He had a position to maintain, and his training focused on strength, confidence and control.

Yet, like a bee to honey, he was intensely attracted to Brenna despite all his efforts not to be and he had no idea how to deal with the feels.

Apparently, his default mode was douchebag.

He'd behaved like a boy with a crush—not the love-sick puppy kind, but the kick-her-shins type. He had no delusions of what Brenna thought of him. She hated him and told him so the summer before she left for university.

The summer he'd had his chance to make things right.

The summer he turned eighteen and realized Brenna was his true mate.

And the summer he'd ruined his chances forever.

More snow drifts moved across his path and blurred his vision. The cold numbed his nose and with the howling wind, his ears couldn't pick up much from his surroundings, essentially rendering him triple-blind. He slowed. The storm, now almost a full-white out, showed no signs of letting up.

Maybe he should turn around and stay at the Jones' cabin. He might not make it back to his parents' place and a cabin was preferable to braving the storm in wolf form.

A strong gust of wind parted the curtain of white and cleared a path ahead. Something red bobbed through the drifts of snow.

What the hell was that?

Eric leaned forward, trying to pick up a scent. Upwind with a strong wind meant he got nothing. Something red and black moved through the snow.

A backpack?

The wind blew hard again, forcing another break in the whiteness, and revealing a solitary figure struggling through the snow drifts with a heavy pack. Who the hell would be out in this crap?

Wolves howled. Not his wolves, not pack. The animals from the forest. They must've caught the hiker's scent. The calls came from both sides of the forest as they closed in on their prey.

Eric snarled and charged forward.

CHAPTER 3

Brenna pushed forward, leg muscles screaming, head pounding and back aching as if one giant bruise covered it. Why on earth had she decided to come to a place where the air hurt her face?

The wolves had caught her scent. She kept moving forward, hoping to lose them with the harsh conditions, but once they got close enough, that plan flew out the window. She hefted her backpack and pressed on. If only she could stall them until she made it to the cabin. She couldn't be too far now.

A black wolf loped along the bank beside her, a gray one mirrored him on the other side.

Her heart beat fast in her chest, and her skin prickled with unease. Damn it, she'd run out of time.

Maisie snarled in her head.

Hey, anytime you want to take over and shift, be my

guest, Brenna snapped, letting years of anger, resentment and disappointment leak into her voice.

Maisie went silent, like she always did.

Fine. Brenna would handle this on her own. She withdrew the long hunter's knife she'd used on her seatbelt and held it out. If she could convince these hungry wolves she was more trouble than a hearty meal was worth, she might have a chance. Things didn't look good. She wasn't useless with a blade, but she wasn't a warrior, either.

Once again, the ache of loss for something she never had punched her stomach. Without a wolf form, Brenna had no natural defence against someone or something bigger or stronger than her. Intelligence only got her so far.

Good brain. The very best brain, Maisie said.

Did you just talk to my brain like a dog?

Maisie gave a mental shrug.

Her wolf's cavalier attitude grated Brenna while her own fear threatened to bubble up and explode. She swallowed and pushed the emotions down. It couldn't help her right now. She couldn't afford to look more like prey than she already did.

"Get back!" she screeched, her lungs screamed from the cold air. Ice had begun to form on the outside of her face covering.

The wolves hopped toward the trees, but kept their eyes trained on her as they continued to pace beside her.

"I'm armed!"

Really? Maisie yawned. *What a ridiculous thing to say.*

Any time, Brenna snarled, reminding her wolf of her role in their predicament.

The wolves wouldn't understand her words, but hopefully the message came across in her tone.

The black one opened its mouth and panted, tongue rolling out a little as if he laughed at her.

Argh.

Sweat lined her winter clothing and her heart raced, but she continued forward. Maybe if she kept yelling at them, she'd make it to the cabin. The cold had soaked to her bones, and her body trembled.

The gray wolf tilted his head back and howled. The pack answered all around her.

Brenna's scalp prickled. She slipped the backpack from her shoulders, letting it fall into the snow with a wet thump and braced for the attack. The wolves launched from the banks and more streamed from the forest toward her.

This was it. Taken out by real wolves. An ironic and insulting way to go.

The candies were a better option, Maisie said.

Brenna crouched and circled slowly, holding her weapon out, trying to gauge which one would reach her first, which side she should defend.

The wolves snarled and rushed toward her.

And skidded to a stop. Silence settled over the

forest as plump snowflakes continued to fall from the angry sky.

A low growl rippled through the air behind her. The hairs on the back of her neck rose and her heart caught in her throat. Brenna turned around slowly. A massive gray wolf stood behind her, his large head a foot from hers. Power radiated from his dense fur. This close and downwind, she should've picked up his scent, but her nose was past the point of numb. It didn't matter. His size and power told her two important things.

Werewolf.

Alpha.

Maisie perked up.

Right, like she'd do anything. Maisie certainly wouldn't use her mysterious powers to drive the transformational process or explain why fate had left Brenna a null instead of a real werewolf like everyone else in her pack.

The wolf pack surrounding them yipped and withdrew into the trees. They didn't stick around or try to test boundaries. Not when confronted with a fullgrown male werewolf. The pack might take him down, eventually, but they'd suffer too many injuries and losses. Wolves were smart. They'd already assessed the cost of this meal too high.

And just like that, the threat on her life was gone... and replaced with a new one.

Her knees threatened to buckle under the alpha's

yellow gaze. He leaned in and sniffed at her covered face. He stilled, remaining motionless as if frozen, except the little puffs of condensed air escaping his snout.

She pulled down her face covering, the icy air sliced her cheeks like shards of glass. "I'm Brenna Jones from the Diamond Pack. Thank you for saving me from the wolves."

The werewolf shook himself from his daze and stepped past her. He leaned down and picked her pack up from the snow before turning back.

"My family has a cabin." She raised her arm and pointed in the direction of her parents' place. Surely this wolf would wonder why she stayed in human form. "I'm a null."

The wolf nodded slowly and stood beside her.

She shrugged and started to walk toward the cabin again. Every muscle in her body screamed.

The wolf growled.

She froze, fear kicking up a notch and threatening to paralyze her. Did she know this wolf? Did he save her from the others just to hurt her himself?

The wolf stepped up beside her again and waited.

"You want me to ride you?" The tension eased away from her shoulders.

Another slow nod.

She hadn't ridden a werewolf since she was a child and her father finally relented after her constant begging. It wasn't a comfortable act for a wolf, their bodies not designed for bearing weight on their backs. But stronger werewolves, like this one, could transport a person or two if they deemed it necessary.

Brenna studied the angry gray skies and the dark clouds moving in. Guess it was necessary. She sheathed her hunting knife, grabbed the pack from the wolf's mouth and stared at his back. With a deep breath, she reached up over the wolf's tall shoulders, clutched handfuls of dense fur and swung up on to the wolf's back.

This day couldn't get any weirder.

CHAPTER 4

Eric charged over the snowbank, urged onward by Brenna's tight grip on his fur. Brenna. She was here, and she was touching him. Voluntarily.

Mate, Brutus growled

The wind howled, and the nasty looking, gray clouds darkened, blotting out the sun and casting them in dark shadows. Eric needed to get her warm, but he also wanted to enjoy this. The moment she found out his identity, she'd recoil with disgust.

Casting them in darkness, the storm intensified instead of letting up. His heart lodged in his throat as each stride sunk his cold paws into deeper and deeper snow. Brenna's warm presence against his back spurred him on. He had to get her to safety.

In the bleary dark, snowbanks and snow-laden trees looked the same. All the same. *Fuck!* His vision strained, but muscle memory and smell directed him through the forest. Eric kept his snout tucked and continued to race through the trenches and over valleys and snow drifts. The other wolves no longer howled. Not anymore. Nothing would be out hunting. Only the sounds of groaning trees and the screaming wind filled Eric's wolf ears. The trip should've taken fifteen minutes.

The wind sliced through his fur and chafed at his hide. His eyes felt as though they blistered. A dark cabin looming in the field of white. Finally. The Jones' cabin.

He charged up the steps to the front entrance, finally stopping where the overhang protected the patio from the snow.

Brenna swung her leg over his shoulders and dismounted. Sort of. More like she fell off. She winced and sucked back air. He leaned forward, trying to offer her help, but she scooted out of his reach.

"I'm fine," she hissed.

Obviously.

In the protected area of the main entrance, Brenna pulled down her face guard again and pursed her lips. Darkness shrouded her fine features, but a trail of dried blood from her forehead and mouth indicated she'd hit her head. He hadn't paused to assess her injuries before taking her to the cabin. His heart beat heavy in his chest. If that twit hadn't lost her gloves...If he hadn't gone for a run...

She sniffed the air around them and her whole body stiffened. Her gaze turned hard. "Eric Buchanan."

He huffed. The jig was up. She'd probably do something stupid now like refuse to go into the cabin or make him freeze outside. He didn't care what she wanted to do, she needed to step inside the cabin and fast. If she'd been in a car accident, she could've sustained a concussion. She might have internal bleeding. She didn't have accelerated healing like him. They needed to assess her wounds and prevent hypothermia from setting in.

Brenna's back straightened and she got that stubborn look to her face, the one where she pressed her full lips into a straight thin line.

Get her safe! Brutus growled. *Protect.*

Knocking her out and hauling her over his shoulder to get her to the cabin seemed a bit barbaric, even if it was for her own safety.

Guess that left the other option. This wouldn't go down well.

The wind picked up, threatening to lacerate them as they had an eye-gazing stand-off. Forcing the tension from his limbs, Eric willed the change.

Brenna threw her hands up and stomped off the patio, probably retrieving the cabin's key from the not so secret hiding place below. She moved less stiffly, but her injuries probably pained her more than she let on.

Pain stabbed at his skin and the tissue beneath. He

condensed and elongated. Bones cracked and organs shifted as his human form spread out and wiped away the wolf. By the time Brenna retrieved the key, he stood in his human skin on the patio.

Naked.

Brenna's glare intensified. The backpack slid from her shoulder and fell into the snow.

"Get inside!" he yelled over the wind. He hopped down the steps into the knee-deep snow to help her up the stairs.

Brenna ignored him and bent to retrieve her backpack.

"Let me take that." He reached for the bag.

Brenna flinched, ducking her head and shying away.

"I'd never hurt you," he said.

Well, he had hurt her, but not physically. He'd never raise a hand to a woman. With a grunt, he snatched the backpack's strap and pulled the bag from her. With the backpack clutched in one hand, he grabbed Brenna's hand and hauled her toward the cabin's door before she could protest or flinch again.

Luckily, she didn't put up a fight. Either too tired, too hurt or too cold, she let him pull her the last few steps to the entrance. She shuffled through the snow, unlocked the door, and yanked on the handle. It didn't budge. Brenna went flying back, ass-first in the snow. She yelped.

"Uh..." He leaned down to help her up, extending

his hand.

She snarled at him.

Okay, then.

He snatched his hand back and turned to the entrance. He ripped the door open and tried to ignore Brenna scrambling to her feet. Without a word, she walked past him into the safety of the cabin. Finally, she was safe. Brutus stopped pacing in his mind and settled while Eric followed her in and shut the door on the blizzard.

Flicking on the lights, the lodgepole pine cabin looked and smelled exactly as he remembered. Basic two-floor layout with bedrooms upstairs, and living room, kitchen and bathroom downstairs. The inside glowed a warm orange as the lights reflected off the interior wood and illuminated the minimal furnishings.

Pine, slightly infused with must, flooded his senses, but the stagnant air contained more warmth than outside.

Brenna fumbled for something in the corner table and turned to face him. He spotted a flash of metal.

The hunting knife.

Seriously?

Not exactly a warm welcome, not that he expected one. After a decade, though, he'd hoped the next time they met, he'd make a better impression. Or at least say something more profound. Anything to make up for what happened.

Now enclosed in the safety of the cabin, her scent

washed over him. The aroma of coffee and candy flooded his senses, along with something else, something more subtle. Roses. As if soft flower petals lifted off the warmth of Brenna's skin, the floral scent caressed his face. He moved closer, wanting to nuzzle into the heat of her body.

He glanced back at her face. Her gaze matched the coldness blowing around them, but her pouty lips, partially open, spoke of wanting something else. Those lips. So close.

She stood near him, her breath coming out in little puffs of white air, as if daring him to laugh or comment. Not happening. Not when she wielded a hunting knife and wanted an excuse to use it on him. He bit his tongue.

Now close and relatively safe, he assessed her condition. The gash on her forehead had stopped bleeding. She moved a bit stiffly. It appeared her injuries were superficial, not life threatening or seriously debilitating. Whatever happened to her, she'd survived. Barely. She was lucky he'd found her when he did.

Protect her, Brutus whined. *Not like other wolves.*

No. Definitely not. Brenna Jones had always marched to her own set of drums, and not just because she was a null. When he discovered his mate was the woman who made his blood sing every time he came near, his emotions collided. He wanted her, but he also expected a powerful wolf as his mate, his equal. Not a null. Not someone more vulnerable and more in need of protection than any other member in the pack. Only after he ruined things past the point of retrieval did he realize Brenna had never been weak and she was already far better than he'd ever hope to be.

And right now, she must be very cold. The winter jacket, toque and face covering were not meant for prolonged excursions through a blizzard and her jeans clung to her legs from the wet snow. They wouldn't have provided much insulation in this weather or protection against the wind.

"Thank you." She stood stiffly and studied him. Her lips compressed into a thin line.

Hell, he was thankful he'd found her when he did. His gut twisted as the "what ifs" flooded his mind again. He dropped the backpack at the entrance. The tension in his legs and torso faded. "You're welcome."

Her gaze flicked down his naked body and back to the door. "You can go now."

Understanding hit him like a semi-truck. "I'm not going out there again."

She flinched.

"Look, Brenna. I know you think little of me and I know you're angry, but I'm not going back to my parents' cabin in this. It's too dangerous to leave you here." And it was fucking cold outside.

Her shoulders drooped. "Find some clothes then and stay away from me."

He saved her life, and she wanted him to leave? To

risk his life again, so she didn't have to be in the same room as him? Unbelievable.

The Brenna he knew throughout high school wouldn't have been so spiteful, so cold. But then, the Brenna he knew was from years ago and he'd hurt her. Maybe he wasn't the only one who'd changed.

"I'll do that. Then I'll get the fire going." His heart felt heavy in his chest. "Did you want to make something warm to drink or take a hot bath?"

Brenna's dark gaze turned to him again and narrowed.

"A bath will help relieve stiff and sore muscles. It looks like you need it." Would probably help melt that cold heart, too. Of course, ice was probably the better option for reducing swelling, but already cold to the bone, the bath would be more relaxing.

"I'll make some hot chocolate," she said, now looking anywhere but at him.

Her tone sounded resigned, but with the one statement, the anger and hurt coursing through his veins eased away. With a momentary truce, Eric set to finding clothes and building a fire. His mind reeled. He'd secretly hoped for an opportunity to be alone with Brenna. He had a lot of groveling to do. Saving her life hadn't thawed any of that ice-cold rage, but now that he had the chance to fix things, did he even want it?

Had he been dreaming of a woman who no longer existed?

CHAPTER 5

Brenna cursed and clanked around the kitchen, putting away the food she'd brought. She stashed the remaining packages of candy hearts. They seemed like such a childish thing, but they were a family tradition for Valentine's. She snuck one last piece and enjoyed the sweet flavour rolling over her tongue.

Had she really suggested Eric go home in a blizzard after he saved her? What was she thinking? Sure, he could shift into a wolf and didn't have to worry about human dangers, like frostbite but the weather was truly nasty. She acted like a spiteful hag, as if being nice to the man would put her in danger of falling for him again. She owed him her gratitude and an apology.

Mate, Maisie whispered.

Brenna shook her head. He'd shut down the possibility of the alpha's powerful son bonding with a weak null years ago. And could she blame him?

Yes.

Yes, she could. He'd decimated her heart before she understood the ramifications. When she turned eighteen a month later and felt the pull and loss of her mate, the awful realization had slammed into her like a sledgehammer. He'd rejected her before she even had a chance. Maybe she would've fought harder had she known. Maybe she would've pulled Anna off him by her hair.

And maybe she would've run away just as she had, just as a null would.

Brenna sighed. That happened so long ago. She learned to live as a wolf-less werewolf. She survived the rejection and learned to live without a true mate. She could learn to be nice.

While she brooded in the kitchen, Eric found a spare set of her brother's clothes and threw them on. He made a roaring fire before going back outside. He said he wanted to get wood for the fireplace and check the perimeter to make sure the wolves hadn't followed them.

An alpha to the core, he probably battled his own overly cautious demons. She'd caught him scanning the interior walls and studying the windows with his hands clenched into fists and his lips pressed tightly together. She didn't need to ask. He'd mentally calculated their vulnerability. The likelihood of a competitive pack infringing on this overlapped areas of their two packs and randomly stumbling upon the alpha's son at her family's remote cabin had to be next to nothing, but Eric knew more about pack politics than she did. Aside from her family, none of whom held prominent positions in the wolf hierarchy, she avoided her own pack.

While Eric tramped around outside, she'd taken a long soak in the bathtub, letting her sore muscles loosen up. She'd cleaned the cut on her forehead, and after staring at her reflection in the bathroom mirror, tension evaporated from her veins. Minor injuries. She'd walked out of that crash with insignificant bumps and bruises.

The bath and moving around had helped with the aches and stiffness. Why did Eric have to be right? It made it more difficult to stay angry at him.

Mate, Maisie whispered.

Shut up.

Brenna set cups down, filled them with chocolate powder, and stirred in the steaming hot water.

Eric had been gone for a while. Had he left? He probably didn't want to hang out with the mate he scorned. They never discussed what happened all those years ago. At the time, there was no need, but now the unspoken words hung heavy in the room. She couldn't read minds or smell emotions like "real" werewolves, but the wary glance he cast over his stiff shoulders before he stomped outside said it all.

Her chest constricted. He might've been a royal

jerk back then, but he didn't deserve to die in a blizzard. She wasn't a twit. Even with her head tucked into the protective shield of Eric's back, the jarring werewolf ride had scared the crap out of her. They'd been lucky to reach her parents' cabin. If he got stuck out there now, he'd have to shift and hunker down.

She bit her lip as she continued to stir the hot chocolate. As much as she hated to admit it, she didn't want to be alone.

She glanced at the door.

Her stomach twisted into a knot. Nausea coiled and threatened to rise. *He better not have left!* Should she go after him? She tossed the idea away before chucking the spoon into the empty sink. If he'd left, there was nothing she could do. Just like she couldn't stop him years ago.

Eric stomped up the stairs outside, and her stomach settled. The door opened, and a burst of bone-chilling, snow-packed air blasted her from across the room. Again, why did she decide to come to a place where the air hurt her face?

Eric slammed the door shut with his foot and set an armful of wet logs by the fire to dry. He must've raided the wood pile by the side of the cabin. He pulled off the ski goggles and cast a wary glance her way—probably in fear of more ice-queen shenanigans—before removing the purple toque. He placed both items by the fire to dry as well.

Her throat grew thick, and words failed her.

Eric slipped out of his borrowed winter jacket and snow pants and hung them on the peg by the door beside her stuff.

Underneath his snow gear, he wore form-fitting dark denim jeans that clung to his powerful thighs and a navy-blue T-shirt with a scuba diving logo, which accentuated his broad shoulders and strong arms.

She swallowed.

The last decade had been kind to Eric, aging him to perfection. Harder edges replaced youthful pretty-boy looks, transforming him into a devastatingly attractive man. The wind-chapped cheeks carved a masculine image, perfected by wind-tussled sandy brown hair. A narrow, straight nose between piercing green eyes, a square jaw with a couple days' worth of stubble, and full kissable lips—Eric Buchanan had become more handsome than he deserved. If Loveable Lumberjacks Magazine wanted a model for their cover, they needed to get a hold of the Topaz pack and book the alpha's son.

His shoulders remained tense. His gaze flicked to her while his mouth flattened. He straightened his tall, fit frame. For the first time since he rescued her, he looked unsure of what to do.

Apologizing for crushing her would be a nice start, but alphas didn't do that whole "sorry" thing.

"Here." She held out a steaming cup of hot chocolate.

Eric nodded and closed the distance to take the

mug from her. His cold hand briefly closed around hers but didn't linger. In fact, he jerked the hot chocolate away so quickly, some of the frothy liquid slopped over the rim.

"Look—" she started.

"Listen—" he said.

She rocked back on her heels, while he ran a hand through his silky hair.

"Ladies first." His voice always had a rough timbre to it, like he was part mountain man. Even when she despised him, she couldn't bring herself to hate his voice. It vibrated along her skin and sank in to warm her bones. It hadn't lost any of its potent power over the years; instead, it had gained new depth.

"I'm sorry," she blurted. "For suggesting you leave. You saved me today and didn't deserve that. Thank you for getting me away from the wolves and bringing me here."

His shoulders relaxed, and his mouth softened. "You're welcome."

They stared at their hot chocolate in silence. At least she did. She couldn't bring herself to maintain eye contact any longer.

"Brenna." He cleared his throat. "I know I hurt you that summer, and I'm sorry."

Shock swept through her body and froze her where she stood. Had she suffered a concussion? Was she hallucinating? Alphas didn't say sorry. As much as she dreamed of this moment, she never expected it to happen.

He waited expectantly.

"I'm sorry, what did you say?" she asked, biting her lip.

He narrowed his eyes at her.

Maisie perked up.

"I'm sorry I was immature, and my actions hurt you. I wish I could change the past."

She wanted to say he hadn't hurt her, that she hadn't cared enough for his actions to cut deep, but that would be a lie. And who was she trying to fool? The apology, though years late, warmed her more than the roaring fire.

"I hope we can use this time to catch up," he continued as if oblivious to the impact of his words. "You might've left without looking back, but I always wondered what happened to you. We have nothing else to do, so why don't you tell me what you've been up to?"

Brenna almost laughed. He thought she hadn't looked back? That she'd gone off without a second thought? That she hadn't figured out what he threw away when she turned eighteen? What would he think if he knew she replayed their first and only kiss more than a few times? More than she cared to admit? That she used that moment, though fleeting and short lived, as a benchmark for all guys? That she sometimes dreamed of confronting him to demand he somehow revoke his refusal of the bond and take her back.

Or beg. She thought about doing that, too.

But even as a null, she had her pride. She had value and she wouldn't, couldn't, bring herself to throw away the last of her dignity.

Instead of laughing, Brenna made the mistake of looking up. Eric's green gaze bore into hers, and something flopped around in her chest. Maybe it was her heart. Maybe it was her resolve to stay pissed at him.

Crap.

Less than an hour with the guy and she was falling under his spell all over again.

This wouldn't do. Despite her dreaming, rejections couldn't be revoked. She might've survived a broken heart once, but that didn't mean she planned on repeating the experience. Ever.

CHAPTER 6

Eric listened to Brenna as she sat on the opposite end of the faded blue couch. She'd curled up to lean against the armrest with her feet tucked under her. Worn jeans and a purple button-down shirt fit her snugly, leaving little doubt to the perfection of her body. She'd cleaned the cut on her forehead and although it looked red and a bit angry, it wasn't deep. Her cheeks flushed with a ruddy red from the harsh conditions outside.

Outside, she'd worn a bulky jacket, and her features had been shrouded in shadow. There'd been no time to truly take in her appearance. Now, in the warm light of the cabin and flickering fireplace, her natural beauty stunned him.

She'd always been good looking, but since he'd last seen her, she'd transformed from a pretty girl with a boyish figure to a remarkable woman. The stylish bob of her white hair framed her pixie nose, pouty full lips, and those large, soulful blue eyes that haunted his dreams. Surrounded by thick dark lashes, her elfin gaze expressed every thought and feeling. She'd be terrible at poker.

As she talked, Eric struggled to keep his gaze from drifting, but occasionally she'd look away or turn, and his gaze travelled down her body, catching a glimpse of her womanly curves before he corrected himself.

Despite his roaming gaze, he hung on every word she said, banking the details to his memory. He knew bits and pieces about her already. He always made a point to ask Brenna's parents about her when he ran into them during their seasonal vacations to the cabin. Though he hadn't seen Brenna in a long time, he still carried the feeling he knew her well.

Mate, his wolf crooned. *Mate, mate, mate, mate—*

Shut up! God, he was sick of listening to his stubborn wolf. Was he the only one plagued with such an ornery beast? Why was the mutt still going on about it, anyway? Brenna refused the mate bond, and he didn't blame her. Neither of them could change the past, but maybe, with time and patience, he could mend their relationship. Maybe even have a friendship. Hell, maybe even more, though he doubted it.

They'd covered the basics. She worked in the health field, he was a project manager for the provincial energy company. He wanted a job where he could move out of the city, and she wanted to travel more. They both lived in Vancouver, only thirty minutes apart. All this time and she lived so close.

One question kept replaying through his mind as she discussed becoming a cardiology technologist, and the places she'd visited when she caught the backpacking bug urging her to discover new places and people. Why had he been such a stubborn jerk?

Why hadn't he chased after her that night ten years ago? Why hadn't he sought her out since then? Why hadn't he pursued her? With or without the mate bond, it wouldn't have mattered. Wolf or no wolf. Eric *liked* her.

"Do you want another hot chocolate?" she asked.

He palmed his warm mug and sat up. "Sure, but why don't I make this round?"

She bit her lip. "No, that's okay. I'll do it."

"Are you sure?" He held out his mug.

Her delicate hand briefly touched his as she took the cup from him. She studied the empty contents but made no move to get up. "I guess I still feel bad about earlier."

He wanted to kiss the frown from her forehead, but such a move would probably be met with a slap to the face, or a punch to the gut. Knowing Mr. Jones, the man would've taught his daughter a thing or two about defending herself, especially after he discovered she couldn't shift.

Besides, Eric wanted her *forgiveness*. Having her apologize to him felt wrong. The uneasy feeling settled around his shoulders like an itchy wool blanket. He stretched his neck, side to side, and tried to shake the feeling.

Oh hell, he wanted a lot more than that.

"So you plan to ply me with chocolate beverages?" he asked, settling back in his seat.

She laughed and stood up. "It's just hot chocolate."

"Said no woman, ever."

She continued to laugh her way to the basic kitchen.

Her hips swayed a little, but not in the over-exaggerated way some women walked to get attention. She moved naturally, confidently.

"Should you text someone to let them know where you are?" she asked over her shoulder. "You can use my phone. It's on the coffee table."

Interesting. Did she wonder if he was married, or had a girlfriend? He sat straighter and waited for Brenna to turn, so he could read her expressive eyes, but she milled around in the kitchen and kept her back to him. He drank in more of her curves, the way her worn jeans hugged her perky butt and shapely thighs.

"No," he answered her. "No girlfriend, wife, or mate, if that's what you're asking." If his parents had their way, things would be different. "But I should let my parents know."

She paused before returning to the task of making hot chocolate, like it was some complicated third-year university chemistry lab experiment instead of mixing powdered chocolate with boiling water.

The sweet aroma of cocoa drifted in the air and blended with the smell of crackling wood from the fire. The heat coiled around him with familiarity. With a resigned sigh, he turned from the woman in the kitchen and plucked Brenna's phone from the table. It still had cell reception, surprisingly, but only two bars. It wouldn't last long. Her dad had texted her to be safe, so she must've already contacted her family. Not wanting to snoop, he left the message unopened and sent a quick text to his parents.

"Your dad replied," he spoke over his shoulder.

"What did he say?"

"Be safe. That's all I saw. I didn't open it."

Brenna made a sound from the kitchen something between a hum and a grunt.

The wind howled through the snow-laden trees outside and rattled the cabin. A finality hung in the air as the storm set in, full force. With the rigid Rockies to the east and the Pacific Ocean to the west, this weather could sit on them for days. Occasionally, an ice-cold draft would slip through the seals of the front door and snake across the room.

He glanced at the phone. No response. One signal bar.

"What about you?" he asked.

"What do you mean?"

"Did you come up here in advance to lay rose

petals on the floor and bed? Do I need to worry about a burly lumberjack barging through the door after tramping through wolf-infested forests during a snowstorm, all for the promise of his lady-love seducing him when he reached the cabin? It is Valentine's Day tomorrow, after all."

Brenna snorted. "Hardly."

Music to his ears.

She headed back to the couch with two steaming mugs. "No, I—"

The lights flickered.

Brenna paused, and looked up. "Oh no."

"I'm surprised it lasted this long," he said. He glanced at the phone again. No response. No bars.

Hopefully, his parents got his message before the reception cut out. Despite their incessant meddling in his love-life, he didn't want them to worry, and he didn't want to offend the Sapphire pack.

"Here, take this," Brenna said. "I'll get the candles and flashlights before—"

As Brenna walked quickly toward him to and hand him the hot chocolate, another hearty gust of wind battered the cabin. The lights winked out.

Brenna gasped, "Oh no!"

CHAPTER 7

Brenna's foot snagged on the carpet. Her body pitched forward, and her heart lodged in her throat. Unable to stop her momentum, her fingers lost their grip on the hot mugs, as she tumbled toward the couch.

The hot chocolate hit Eric first.

He howled.

Her body impacted next. Her chest slapped against his chocolate-soaked T-shirt and hard body. With whip-like action, her head snapped forward and smacked Eric's temple.

Pain flared across her forehead. The backs of her eyes throbbed.

"Oooooh," she groaned. She tried to roll off Eric to sit by his side, but his arms circled around her.

"Ouch." Eric's deep voice vibrated in her ear. "You pack quite the punch...with your head."

"I'm so sorry. How burnt are you?" She cringed inwardly. Maybe she should get off him first and give him a chance to check. What was it about this guy that made her turn into a fumbling, bumbling teenager all over again?

His arms tensed around her, but he didn't let go. "I'll live. I have to admit, the aftercare saved me."

Aftercare? Bonking heads? Since when was that a good thing? She rubbed her forehead. "Sorry about that, too. My mom always said I had a hard head."

"Probably a good thing, considering how much you've smacked it around today. Are you okay?"

"Yeah. Think my pride is more bruised."

His chest rumbled as he chuckled. The action rubbed her breasts and sent a lightning bolt to her core.

"I don't have the agility of a true werewolf," she rambled on. "I was always so clumsy compared to the rest of the pack. That always bothered me."

"You're a true werewolf."

"I'm a null."

"Doesn't matter."

"It did to you."

Eric opened his mouth to object, but snapped it shut instead. Because she was right, and he knew it.

A sharp pain pinched her heart and she scrambled to get up.

Stay! Maisie whined.

Eric's arms tightened at first, as if he would fight to keep hold, but his muscles relaxed, and he released her.

"For the record, when I said I enjoyed the aftercare I wasn't talking about your head-butt," he said, his voice more gravelly than usual, as if it had churned in a cement mixer before coming out.

Brenna sucked in a breath. Her heart beat so loudly, he could probably hear it from where he sat, a foot away. Warmth radiated from his body. With the flickering light from the fireplace, Brenna looked down at Eric. She wanted to run her hands down his chocolate-splattered chest—the same hard packed muscles that had pressed against her moments before.

She also wanted to throttle him. He hadn't denied her null comment. He simply didn't address it at all.

"Um, Brenna?" Eric's voice interrupted her thoughts. "The candles? Do you need help finding them?"

She stood in front of him with her legs shoulder width apart and her hands on her hips. He'd essentially have to bowl her over if he wanted to get up.

"Right! Stay there. Let me get the candles and flashlights." She ducked down and used the limited light from the fireplace to find the two, now-empty, mugs on the floor.

"Okay," Eric said.

He sounded amused, but when she turned from where she crouched on her hands and knees, shadows shrouded his face. Her gaze drifted down the outline of his strong body. His pants looked tighter, as if...

She sprang up and clutched the mugs to her chest.

She'd better find some alternative light sources fast because the firelight played tricks on her mind.

CHAPTER 8

E ric cleaned the sticky mess in the living room while Brenna searched for candles and more flashlights. His pants had grown uncomfortably snug. Not entirely his fault.

Brenna had been on her hands and knees before him with her tight ass turned up, swaying as she fumbled for the mugs. Now, the very memory made him hard, like some awkward, pimple-faced freshman with no experience.

Well, he certainly wasn't a saint, nor inexperienced, but the image burned into his memory. It set his imagination running to the nearest gutter to slop around. How he'd love to grip those hips and...

Eric cursed and readjusted his pants. Again.

Why hadn't he said something when she called him out? Spoken up? Even tried to deny it? He had thought of her differently as a null, but not in the way she probably thought. She didn't have the enhanced strength, agility or accelerated healing like a werewolf who could shift, and when he was a teenager, he thought that made her weak. Vulnerable. But not in a mean way. He wanted to protect her. Life as a werewolf was difficult. Life as the alpha's mate was downright dangerous. How could he place her in that role when she didn't have the same arsenal of skills to defend herself?

Only after he lost her did he realize she had her own strength, and he could be strong enough for both of them and physically protect her.

Of course, he hadn't thought any of that through. Instead, he'd made a knee jerk reaction and in that one cowardly, adolescent moment of stupidity, he'd ruined everything. And when the opportunity arose to explain, to apply a calming salve to the wound he inflicted, he'd commented on her hot chocolate body slap instead.

Eric squeezed the sponge, dirty water smelling of chocolate splattered against the floor. He groaned and squatted to quickly wipe it up. He'd successfully mopped up the floor in the limited light and cleaned the couch as best he could. The sweet aroma of chocolate still drifted off the worn blue fabric of the cushions.

He glanced down.

Or maybe the smell came from him. He chucked the chocolate-soaked sponge into the kitchen sink and peeled off his shirt and sticky jeans. He used the last of the water in the tank to wash them in the sink.

Luckily, the cabin's supply room held multiple large jugs of drinking water. With the power out, the electrically-powered pump couldn't refill the tank that supplied the cabin. The Jones family might have a generator, but the last thing Eric wanted to do in the middle of the night during a storm was tramp around in thigh-deep snow to find it.

Eric plunged his clothes in the sink water one last time before twisting them to remove the excess water.

He carried the shirt and jeans to the fire and hung them by the fire. The crackling flames had burnt a little low, so he threw another log on the fire.

Clean room? Well, close enough. Check.

Clean clothes? Check.

Clean Eric? He ran his hands down his chest. Sticky.

Footsteps thumped down the stairs from where the bedrooms were, and the light from a flashlight bounced along the wall before flooding the stair landing. Here came Brenna, and he wore boxer-briefs, and nothing else. He glanced at the couch. The one towel he'd found earlier currently soaked up the excess water he'd used to clean up the couch.

When the light turned from the stair landing and illuminated him from the darkness, like a giant spot-light, Brenna gasped. "Why are you naked?"

CHAPTER 9

The candles Brenna had tucked under her arms and clasped in her hand fell to the floor in a clatter.

Broad shoulders, chiseled abs, a defined V of muscle and a trail of dark brown hair led to fitted black boxer-briefs with a definite bulge, left little to Brenna's imagination. Not that she needed one. She'd seen him completely naked earlier. The circumstances hadn't allowed her to appreciate what Eric freely showed. An image flashed through her mind, one of her peeling down the elastic waistband of those briefs while tasting his skin and trailing the rippling muscles with her tongue.

The heady scent of the burning logs and unlit candles along with her imagination of what could transpire left her head spinning.

"Well," Eric crooned. "I'm *almost* naked because

this beautiful woman dumped hot chocolate all over my clothes."

"Yes, I did." Her heart raced and her cheeks heated as she continued to rake his body with her gaze. Thank goodness she hid behind the light of the flashlight.

"Yes, you did," he said.

"Are you okay? The hot chocolate was pretty hot." Sure he might heal fast, but that didn't make him a masochist. She scooped up the fallen candles, taking the time to get a hold of herself.

Eric turned to her, giving her memory a full frontal view to archive. "I'm fine. Though I wonder now if you did it on purpose."

"I did no such thing." She tucked the last candle under her arm and straightened.

"No? My mistake. Though we both know I deserved it."

She took a deep breath and willed her gaze away from his naked body. Sweat prickled along her skin while Maisie kept howling inappropriately in her head. Brenna intended to keep hating him and wanting to slap her naked body against his wasn't exactly going to help. Nothing would happen between them and the sooner she accepted that, the sooner she could move on. "Are you going to put something on?"

Eric grinned, flashing even white teeth. "For someone shocked and insulted by my near-naked state, you're certainly keeping the spotlight on me." He held his hand, palm out, as if to block out the light.

She aimed the flashlight at the couch. "Sorry." Forcing her gaze away from his rippled abs, again, she took in the couch. He'd cleaned up. Nice. She hadn't looked forward to dousing the couch to get the hot chocolate out. She'd assumed he'd leave it to her. Most of the men she dated would have.

"You're not forgiven," he said.

Her muscles tensed. "Huh?"

Eric ran his hand down his bare chest. "I'll forgive you for trying to scald off my first layer of skin *after* you help me finish cleaning up the mess you made."

"Looks like you've already done a good job."

"Brenna?"

She kept her gaze pasted on the couch. "Yes?"

"I'm still dirty."

She turned the flashlight back to him. He squinted in the light, but it did little to deter his cheeky grin.

"Dirty mind, maybe," she muttered.

His sexy mouth twitched, and his grin widened. "Give me a sponge bath?"

Need flooded her body, and her stomach lurched with need. Inwardly, her mind screamed, "Yes, yes, yes!" But she kept her mouth firmly shut and stalked to the kitchen to place the candles on the counter. She set them down, one by one, on the granite surface and took deep breaths in between.

"Are you okay?"

"Of course. Why do you ask?"

"You're very aggressive with your candle placement."

Aggressive with her candle placement? Really? She sputtered. How dare he critique her ability to handle a candle? She squeezed her eyes shut for a moment. That wasn't what bothered her.

How dare he proposition her now? He had his chance.

"Here," she said, and plucked a soaked sponge from the sink. "Let's compromise." She chucked the sponge at him from across the room. Thanks to high school softball, and social adult leagues, her aim was spot on. Eric laughed as he caught it.

"Fair enough," he said.

He ran the wet sponge over his corded muscles, the trail of moisture evident in the flickering light from the fireplace.

She tore her gaze away and turned back to the kitchen. Bracing herself on the counter, she took a few deep breaths to calm her raging libido. She hated Eric.

Didn't she?

Focus, Brenna.

Light the stupid candles. Ignore the temptation vibrating from the six feet of sexual energy a few feet away—the one who currently lathered himself with a wet sponge in front of a roaring fireplace while he watched her with a glint in his eye. Damn it! He must know the effect he had on her. He had full werewolf abilities. He'd detect her increased heartrate, her faster breathing, and her arousal.

She cringed.

After searching a few drawers, Brenna found the matches. She milled around, lighting candles and placing them in the kitchen and living room. The soft light flooded the cabin, adding shadows and the soft fragrance of vanilla. She didn't use all of them. The candles and flashlight batteries needed to last. They might be holed up here for days.

Days.

Alone with Eric Buchanan in a candle-lit, secluded cabin.

Another deep breath.

She switched off the flashlight and turned to Eric.

He sat in front of the fire, leaning back and supporting himself with his arms. The light from the roaring fire licked his chest and highlighted his well-defined abs.

As if he sensed the weight of her attention, he turned, and his green gaze locked with hers. Images overtook her mind—their naked bodies entangled in the dancing light of the fire, his hard body pressed against hers, Eric leaning back wearing the same content expression he wore now as she straddled him.

Maisie prodded her brain. *You could have that.*

Brenna squeezed her thighs together as heat pooled between her legs—legs she'd like him to part with his hands before delving his tongue—

"Brenna?" Eric called to her. "Join me?" He patted the space on the rug beside him.

She didn't like Eric Buchanan. He broke her heart.

Maisie snorted. *Get over it already.*

I'll never have a true mate because of him, and nothing we do now will change that.

Meh, Maisie managed to pour a physical shrug into her voice. *You weren't true mates with those other guys you brought to our bed.*

Brenna sighed, ignored the werewolf, and walked over to Eric. If they didn't have history, she probably wouldn't hesitate to join him, even if it was only for a physical liaison, and not a relationship or a promise of one. Girls had needs, too.

But she had history with Eric.

They hadn't dated. One serious conversation followed with his...

Brenna shook her head. She'd fallen for his charm.

After nursing a raging crush on him for all through high school, she forgave him for the years of torment after one well-acted "heartfelt" confession and apology. She completely fell for his, "I'm a different person" routine. Then, he proved he was exactly who she originally thought—a playboy jerk. An alpha's arrogant son who deemed himself too important and powerful to slum it with a null. A month later, when she turned eighteen and felt the tug of the bond, she realized the extent of his rejection.

She sat down beside said jerk, crossed her legs, and

leaned back. The heat of the fire rolled over her and her chocolate-soaked clothes. She should probably clean them as Eric had, but that would involve undressing.

She wasn't the same person she was in high school. Maybe Eric had grown as well. Her parents certainly thought well of him, though they didn't know their history. No one did. Too mortified to share how her true mate didn't want a null, she'd kept the truth a secret. She avoided this cabin, this place, leaving after high school and never looking back. But her family vacationed and stayed in touch with Eric's parents, wanting to stay on friendly terms with the larger, more powerful pack. Mom and Dad gushed and regaled her with the latest information on Eric, painting him as an accomplished gentleman.

Maybe the reality matched the fantasy she'd created over the years.

She glanced over to find him studying her with those green eyes.

Maybe he'd finally grown up.

They shared a smile.

He straightened and leaned forward.

Her heart leapt into her chest, her breath staggered and paused. What would she do if he tried to kiss her?

"Not a lot to do in a secluded cabin," she blurted. Her heart continued to race. The fire became too hot. Little pebbles of sweat broke out across her nose.

Eric stilled. With his thoughts private, his mouth twisted up, he sat back. "What were you going to do?"

Rip his underwear off and ride him like a bronco?

She bit the inside of her cheek and stared at the fire. "What do you mean?"

"What had you planned to do up here on your own? We already ruled out the randy lumberjack."

Ironic words, since aside from the facial hair and lack of plaid, Eric reminded her of a lumberjack. What had she planned? This weekend was supposed to consist of three things: reading romance novels, eating candy, and feeling sorry for herself.

Maisie decided now would be a good time to pipe up. *You were going to read smut and touch yourself.*

Her face heated. Busted. By her own little internal devil.

"Read," she answered, her voice growing thick. "But the books are in the back of the truck with my clothes." *Along with my vibrator...*

Eric's gaze bore into her as he studied her. Did he detect her secret plans? Could he see the blush burning her cheeks? Smell her arousal? Silence fell over them as the wind continued to howl. The force of the storm rattled the cabin.

"I only took the food and survival gear with me," she said.

"There are other things we can do." His rough voice broke the moratorium and left little room for misinterpretation.

"Huh." Her gaze drifted down his body again. Was she seriously considering it? Having sex with the mate who abandoned her seemed like an ill-advised choice, yet...

Eric shrugged. "If you want to sit around and read from the one book in the entire cabin instead, I'll support that decision."

The Encyclopedia of Mythical Creatures? Brenna snorted. Not fucking likely.

A mean burst of wind shook the cabin. In the distance wolves howled, or maybe it was the storm. No wildlife would venture out in this crap. The lights flickered on, then promptly shrouded them in fire-lit darkness again.

She laughed, and they shared another look. She froze as his gaze sparkled from the firelight and flickering candles. Her body warmed from more than the fire. She mulled over the decision.

It's just sex, Maisie whispered. *You don't need to like him to have an orgasm.*

I don't have casual relationships, she fired back.

Exactly! That's why you haven't gotten laid in eons. Imagine how good it will feel.

He chose to have sex that night with Anna, not me. He knew I was his mate and turned me down.

That was ten years ago. He's had sex with plenty of women since then. He's experienced. He'll know what he's doing. And if you don't like him, you don't have to see him ever again. He can't scorn his true mate more than once, anyway. That's already been done. You have nothing to lose and a whole lot of orgasms to gain.

Brenna huffed, momentarily at a loss for words, or argument.

As if sensing her inner turmoil, Eric relaxed. He reached out and ran a finger down her face.

"I never slept with Anna," he said.

Maisie stilled before fading out. Brenna's brain shut down. She turned to him, mouth agape. "What?"

CHAPTER 10

Eric enjoyed watching Brenna's best fish-out-of-water impression. Her confusion wiped away quickly, as a look of relief played across her pixie features. Her expressive face read like a book. The hunger burning in her gaze earlier hadn't been a figment of his imagination, nor were the flashes of doubt. He needed to clear up their past.

"I never slept with Anna," he repeated. "Not that night. Not ever."

"But I thought—"

"I know what you thought, and I let you think it. I was eighteen. I didn't know how I felt about finding my true mate so quickly. I thought I'd have time. When you walked in on Anna throwing herself on me, I went with it. I didn't sleep with her, though, and as soon as you left, I wished I could take everything back. I wanted to make it right, but I was too late."

Back then, not everyone had a cell phone. Certainly not Brenna Jones. When he realized his mistake, he'd sought her out, only to learn from her parents she'd left for university and had met some guy during orientation week. The news gutted him. The words still haunted his dreams.

Werewolves gained the ability to sense their true mates at eighteen. Brenna had her birthday, realized the depths of his actions, discarded the bond, and left without a second thought. It still cut, but he had no one to blame but himself.

"Too late?" she said.

"You were dating someone. Josh something-or-other. Your parents seemed to like him." Well damn, his tone came out a bit more bitter than he'd like.

She didn't comment, but a wry smile spread across her face as if recalling a funny memory. He didn't care about past boyfriends. He cared about now. They sat in silence while he watched the wheels turn in her head.

"You spoke to my parents?" she asked.

"I wanted to find you to explain things, but you'd already moved on."

Brenna studied her hands in her lap. How he wanted to pick them up and place them on his body, feel her wanting him as much as he wanted her.

"I thought about you," she said.

"You did?"

She nodded. "Thought about what a jerk you were, and how I'd fallen for your act."

He winced. "It wasn't an act."

"How do I know this isn't an act, too? You're very charming."

He clenched his teeth, and his hands balled into fists. "I'm not playing around, Brenna."

She flinched before turning that large soulful gaze on him. "Not now, I get that, but can you understand how much you hurt me?"

He nodded. Against every alpha instinct in his body, he went for honesty, accepting the truth and owning his mistakes. She deserved that. "You'd confronted me at a party and told me I'd been a jerk to you throughout high school. I acknowledged my stupidity and apologized for it. I explained I treated you that way because I really liked you. You admitted when I wasn't a jerk, you really liked me, too. I believe you mentioned a 'passionate girl crush.' We made out. Things got intense. By that point, I realized you were my mate but knew you wouldn't feel the pull until your birthday. You went to call your brother to let him know you'd walk back to the cabin with friends, and when you came back, you found Anna Walker kissing me."

"The same Anna Walker you'd been dating, and rumour had it she planned to lose her virginity to you at that party." She jabbed a stiff finger into his chest.

He chuckled. "Well, one, she was no virgin, and two, we'd broken up the weekend before, but she plotted to seduce me and get me back."

"She was in her bra and panties sucking the life out of your face while dry-humping your leg."

"Yeah." He scratched his jaw. "By the time I untangled myself from that girl's clutches to talk to you, you were gone. I don't blame you. I hate myself."

Brenna huffed.

"It seems our lives have been entangled with misunderstandings and hurt. At least where you and I are concerned," he said. "For what it's worth, I wish I could take it back."

"Yeah," she whispered. "Me too."

He leaned forward, drawing in her rosy scent. "Let me make it up to you."

She took a deep breath and turned to him. With her shoulders pulled back, she met his gaze. Those pouty lips parted, and his stomach lurched. She was going to deny him again, and it would be final this time. Before, the needling doubt had also meant a glimmer of hope. Even though she rejected the bond, they could still build something, something true without the bond. If she denied him now, though, it would close the door on possibilities between them forever.

"Okay," she said.

CHAPTER 11

For a dazed second, Brenna's breath caught in her throat as Eric sat beside her, blinking. Maybe he hadn't heard what she said? Maybe he already changed his mind? How exactly did he plan to make it up to her anyway?

Without warning, his large hands gripped her arms and pulled her roughly to him. Her breasts smushed against his hard chest. Her heart pounded against her ribcage. He leaned in, and his mouth crushed hers.

Maisie trilled with excitement.

Full lips warmed hers as his hot tongue slipped inside her mouth. This kiss was nothing compared to the one from ten years ago. This kiss put the other one, the kiss she'd held on a pedestal and used as a benchmark for the last decade, to shame.

A storm built inside her to match the one outside.

Her blood turned molten as it flowed through her veins.

Eric explored her face and neck with his mouth as he roamed her body with his hands.

She wanted more. She wanted to touch and taste, somehow erase their painful past and create a new one. She snuck her hands up his torso and splayed them against his hard chest. His heartbeat pounded against her open palm.

Did their history matter? Not right now. The mating call was gone, but that didn't mean they couldn't enjoy each other's company. Who cared what happened after they left the cabin? Brenna certainly didn't. Not at this moment. Not with his tongue tracing a swirling path down her neck.

Eric suddenly pulled back with a groan, tugging her bottom lip with his teeth.

The sexual fog lifted from her senses and the surrounding environment refocused. Wood burned in the fireplace, cracking and popping as the heat laved her skin. The occasional cold draft from the poorly sealed windows and doors snaked across the room, the faint smell of dish soap used to clean the couch and Eric's clothes, the vanilla candles, the howling wind blasting through the surrounding forest outside... One sense overpowered it all.

Taste.

The taste of Eric's chocolate-infused mouth coated her tongue.

Eric must've forgotten whatever it was he planned to say because he was kissing her again and making her senses sing. Her eyes started to drift shut as she enjoyed the lingering flavour teasing her taste buds.

Something large and furry crashed through the window, spraying the room with glass shards. Eric ripped his face away from hers and jumped to his feet. A wolf straightened from the ground, snarled at them, and launched into the air, straight for Brenna.

Eric moved in time to intercept the large furry wolf flying through the air. Not a normal wolf. A werewolf. His unfamiliar scent slapped her in the face. The two crashed to the floor by Brenna's feet and rolled. The werewolf's teeth snapping the empty air, inches from Eric's face. He wouldn't have time to shift to protect himself.

Heart in her throat, Brenna raced to the back room. Her brother used to stash a .22 rifle in the cold storage room, defying Canadian gun laws. She stumbled into the dark room and groped the shelf, ignoring the snarls from the other room. Her fingers ran along the cold surface of the rifle's stock. She snatched the gun and grabbed a handful of rounds. Some fell from the shelf and tinkled as they hit the tiled floor.

She shoved the extra bullets in her pocket and slid the first round in the chamber. A single shot, bold action rifle against an angry unknown werewolf. What could go wrong?

Everything.

But she just had to distract the wolf long enough for Eric to shift. She couldn't hear him yelling and growling anymore.

She ran back in the room. The werewolf hunched over Eric. Blood was everywhere. She pushed the bolt forward and snapped it down. Locking the rifle into her shoulder, she held the rifle firmly, flicked the safety, aimed, and pulled the trigger. With a .22 calibre, the rifle didn't kick back, but the sound still punched her eardrums. The werewolf yipped and jumped back.

With shaking hands, Brenna pulled back the bolt. The empty casing flew out and clattered to the ground. She dug out another round and chamber. The werewolf snarled and stalked toward her. Eric lay prone in a pool of his blood by the fireplace. He wasn't shifting. Why wasn't he moving?

Why wasn't the beast attacking? The wolf had stopped snarling and shook his head.

Brenna lifted the rifle and fired again. Too wide, the bullet grazed the wolf's haunches. She had too much adrenaline rushing through her veins. She needed to breathe. Focus. Ignore the fear and take aim properly.

The werewolf glanced over his shoulder briefly before refocusing on her, stalking forward again. He still hadn't attacked. What was wrong with him? He was huge with the typical gray wolf colouring but stood nearly twice the height and width of a normal wolf, he radiated power and intimidation. With matted fur and a tangy scent, he trained his cold gaze on Brenna and snarled. His fangs dripped with saliva and Eric's blood.

A feral.

Nothing else explained this attack. No pack. No motive. No sense. Ferals attacked humans and other werewolves indiscriminately until they got put down. Nothing and no one could calm their rage. This one should've already lunged at her, but as if invisible ropes held him back, he remained put, alternating between shaking his head and growling.

Brenna pulled another bullet out of her pocket. It slipped from her fingers and fell, clinking as it bounced off the hard wood floor. Ice clamped her spine. She pulled another round from her pocket. Gripping it tightly, she placed it in the chamber, slid the bolt forward, took a breath and aimed on her exhale. The bang of the shot filled the cabin. The bullet pegged the werewolf square in the forehead. The wolf's head snapped back.

Brenna lowered the rifle.

The wolf's head lowered. An angry red wound marked the center of his forehead. She hit him between the eyes in the T-zone. The wolf staggered. The bullet had bounced off his supernatural skull and though it phased him, it wouldn't down him.

Brenna reloaded. She had nowhere to run to. Nowhere to hide. She tried to peer around the hulking werewolf to locate Eric. No luck.

The wolf straightened. He narrowed his cold eyes

at her and leaned back, loading his weight on his hindquarters.

Oh no.

Brenna raised the gun and sighted her shot as the wolf lunged forward.

Another wolf slammed into the side of the feral one. Eric! The two large wolves, evenly matched in size, rolled over one another, crashing into the couch and side table. Wood splintered and fractured. Fur flew as teeth snatched and claws shredded.

The feral pushed off Eric, a chunk of his hide and flesh caught in Eric's mouth. The feral yipped as his flesh tore.

Brenna stood to the side of the room, rifle still in her hand, and watched. What else could she do? She couldn't take another shot at the feral without risking hitting Eric. Besides, Eric looked like he had recuperated from his wounds and was currently winning.

With a flurry of fur, the feral growled and lunged away from Eric. His paws and claws clattered and scraped against the slick hardwood floor as he fought for traction.

Brenna lifted the rifle, paused to aim, and shot him in the hindquarters.

The werewolf yelped. After gaining purchase, he ran across the room, knocking over another side table. The lamp crashed the floor, spraying glass, but the feral didn't pause. He kept barrelling through the cabin until he jumped out the window he'd come in through.

Still in wolf form, Eric dropped the hunk of feral flesh at her feet and panted.

"Ew."

He licked her face.

"Gross."

He whined.

She jerked her head toward the window. "Go."

Eric smiled in wolf form, flashing his shiny teeth and took off after the feral. She knew what had to be done. Eric had to hunt down and kill the feral, putting him out of his own misery and keeping everyone else on the mountain safe. If he didn't, the feral would continue to terrorize any human or werewolf he encountered and he most definitely would return to try his luck against Eric and Brenna again.

Brenna sighed and lowered the rifle. The tension flowed from her muscles and the effect from adrenaline racing through her veins faded. She wanted a nap, but one look at the destroyed living room and she knew she had a lot of work to do. Besides, she wouldn't rest until she knew Eric was safe.

CHAPTER 12

In naked human form, Eric walked through the front door just as Brenna finished sweeping up the rest of the glass. Luckily, Brenna's family had extra boards, nails, and a hammer for emergencies. After locating the supplies, she nailed the board to the windowsills to seal up the broken window. A new draft snuck in through the cracks, but this cabin always had an energetic air flow.

Relief swept through Brenna at the sight of Eric, fully healed and safe.

He shut the door against the cold and searched the room with a wild gaze. Feral wild. Oh no.

Sometimes, the hunt drove the inner beasts too much. All werewolves drove a fine line between the wild animal they housed inside and their humanity. All werewolves fought to keep control. Once they tipped over the edge and became feral, nothing could save them. Had Eric lost the battle?

The moment Eric spotted her, the tension from his shoulders eased and he stalked toward her. Another intense emotion replaced the wild gaze. With fluid grace, he moved like the predator he was, prey in sight. "I need you."

She lowered the dustpan to the nearby coffee table and leaned the broom against the wall. Eric's words rocked her, they called to her, caressed her, demanded her.

Eric stopped a few feet in front of her, his gaze boring into hers.

What was he waiting for? Consent? He saved her from a feral werewolf. Her lips still prickled from his kiss. Her body yearned for more and her heart pulsed. She *ached* for him. "Well, I don't know. You were gone for a while."

Eric pursed his lips.

"Us fickle women just..." She snapped her fingers. "Change our minds without—"

Eric was on her before she could finish her sentence. His hot mouth claimed hers, his strong arms crushing her body to his. He stole her breath away but before she suffocated, he pulled back and traced her lips with the tip of his finger. "I like you like this."

"Alive."

"Safe. Warm. In my arms..." His voice trailed off as he leaned in farther to kiss her neck.

"And?"

"I want you naked."

Her heartbeat sped up, and her ears filled with white noise. Was she really going to do this?

He straightened, and his green gaze held her in place, questioning. Even now, when his wolf rode him hard to take, he waited.

Despite her nerves, her skin danced, begging for his touch. His calm, yet anxious, presence reassured her. His expression open, his demeanor accepting. She took a deep breath and met his gaze.

Slowly, he plucked open her purple, chocolate-soaked shirt, one button at a time. The absence of his mouth and hands on her skin gave her chills, but she didn't care. Her nerves sang on high alert. She watched, mesmerized as Eric unwrapped her.

Her shirt draped open and Eric sucked in a breath. The bra she'd chosen that morning, more for function-ality than seduction, did little to dampen the fire in his gaze. He pushed the cups down, dragging the edges against her nipples and let her breasts spill out.

Eric licked his lips and leaned forward.

When his hot mouth clamped on her, she moaned. Her head dropped back, and she closed her eyes. She'd dreamt of this moment many times. Always, she'd awaken in desperate need, only to chas-tise herself for dreaming about *him*. This moment with the real Eric made her wicked dreams, the ones with images so vivid and real she'd call out in the middle of the night, seem like faded black and white remakes.

Eric's lips, mouth, and tongue continued to explore as he removed more clothing and lowered her to the rug in front of the fireplace—the one covering the new blood stains in the wood. As his hands roamed the curves of her body, stirring the internal ache, he peeled off her remaining clothes. Her body melded to his as the nearby fire's intensity licked her skin.

Eric's touch sought out, and found, the sensitive zones on her body, as if he alone held the key, and the blueprint to her cravings. Any stiffness remaining in her body from the accident dissolved out of her limbs as she turned to a puddle of molten lava. He kissed around her bruises and continued to move down. When his head ducked between her legs, waves of delight rippled through her body. Her eyes popped open, and her vision swam.

Oh, my. Yes!

She moaned again, as she melted into pure bliss. Waves of pleasure rolled through her body, yet she wanted more.

Her skin tingled, playing the tune Eric wrought from her body. He covered her body with his once more, and while she reeled from her first orgasm, he pushed slowly inside. When he joined his body with hers in perfect harmony, he answered the ache within. The intense heat built again as he stoked the fire and continued to pump his hips and thrust deep inside.

Pressed together, she moved with him, her heart thudding against her chest. She held on, clutching him tight, never wanting to let go. Never wanting this delicious moment to end yet yearning for release.

As the pressure increased, no thoughts plagued her mind. No worries, no concerns; instead, a sense of belonging, of being complete and consumed with exquisite satisfaction. Brenna sank her nails into Eric's back as she came again, so intense light splintered across her vision and she bit into his shoulder. Eric groaned as he found his own release, his body tense and slick with a fine sheen of sweat.

Brenna peeled her nails from his skin and smoothed the indents with her hands as if it would make the wounds she'd inflicted magically disappear. Eric's weight pressed her into the floor as he sagged on top of her. She didn't mind. She liked it. Unclamping her teeth, she kissed the unintentional bite marks with zero regrets from losing control.

CHAPTER 13

In a dazed state of contentment, Brenna lay cocooned under the weight of Eric's body. When he shifted to gently pull out and lay beside her, the cooler air prickled her skin and washed her senses with the sweet tang of pine and vanilla. She sat up, threw another log on the fire, and pulled her knees to her chest.

The soft rug brushed her bum and legs.

She'd had sex with Eric Buchanan. The alpha mate who'd felt their mate bond and decided he didn't want it.

Instead of a rapidly beating heart, or an insatiable need to hide or flee, her muscles remained languid, not stiff. Her body became consumed with an odd, prickling warmth spreading across her chest and radiating out to her limbs. Everything felt right. As if this was how things should be. And prior to the rejection, this was how things should've, could've, been.

She sighed and ignored he painful ache in the pit of her stomach. What was the point of mourning something that never happened?

Eric pulled himself up to sit beside her. After a couple of sideways glances, he scooted closer until his bare shoulders nudged hers.

"So," he said.

"So," she said, heart hammering in her chest. "That happened."

"Yup."

She continued to let the hot air flow over her naked skin, enjoying the heat of the fire. "Are you still injured from the fight?"

He patted his rock hard abs. "Good as new."

He was better than good, but he didn't need her to feed his ego. "The feral?"

"Taken care of."

She nodded, not wanting more detail other than confirming the threat was neutralized.

They watched the fire crackling and burning. The candles burned mid-way and gently wafted soft scents in their direction as the time passed. Five minutes? Twenty? It felt like forever. With each strained second of silence, Brenna's heart slowed and plummeted in her chest. Self-doubt replaced her original contentment. Had this been a mistake?

This would be an awkward weekend if he wanted

nothing to do with her now that he'd gained another conquest.

Nothing to do with her?

Her stomach twisted into a knot.

She didn't want this to end. She'd didn't want this feeling to be unreciprocated, to have this relationship end with an awkward silence as the punctuation mark.

Eric cleared his throat. "I have a question."

Oh dear god. What could he possibly want to know that she hadn't told him with her body? "Yes?"

"When can we do that again?"

A weight lifted from her shoulders. She turned to Eric. His mouth twisted up in a wide grin, and his green gaze twinkled in the firelight.

She licked her lips.

His gaze followed the movement and he leaned in to kiss her gently. Any remaining tension from her self-doubt dissipated from her muscles, replaced with thrumming in her veins.

Pulling back enough to speak, his lips continued to brush hers. "There are things I want to do to you."

"Oh?"

"Mmmm." He kissed her again. "Naughty things. Very bad things. Sexual things."

"I'm listening." She caught his lips with hers and kissed him back.

He pulled her onto his lap and deepened the kiss.

His tongue delved in as he grew hard beneath her.

"I want to bend you over something..." he said between head-dizzying kisses.

"Still listening."

He continued to whisper a long list of all the things he'd like to do.

She squirmed on his lap, his words and tongue creating a dizzying effect. Her heart beat heavy, punching her ribcage while Eric whispered his naughty intentions.

The ache inside her increased to an almost unbearable throbbing. She reached between them to grip his shaft. She stroked it. He was so hard, it pulsed.

"I want you screaming my name," he whispered into her ear before he began to travel down her neck with his mouth.

She shifted her body, so she hovered over him. He gripped her hips, and she guided him in.

"I want you," he said. He captured her mouth again with his as he thrust his hips up and pulled her down. "I want you to be mine."

Why would he tease her with these words? She would've already been his had he not been an idiot all those years ago. She ground against him. "You know what I want?"

"What?" he groaned and trailed hot kisses along her shoulder as she began to move.

She rocked her hips, adding to the aching need building in her core. "First, I want to ride you until you scream *my* name." She used his hair to pull his head back. His gaze twinkled as it met hers, and his mouth parted. She crushed her lips against his. The rough callouses of his hands dug into the soft flesh of her hips as he clutched her and helped create a perfect rhythm.

As the inferno grew and stars swam in her vision, she realized she might've already given him his wish.

As the storm raged through the night and next day, Brenna happily helped tick off Eric's list of wants, as well as some of her own. With no sign of the blizzard letting up, it looked as though they might make it through the sexual marathon his imagination had planned.

Hours later, content and spent, they lay entangled on a bed in one of the upstairs rooms.

"Happy Valentine's Day," Eric said as he trailed kisses up her body, which gleamed with a light sheen of sweat. The soft cotton sheets stuck to the underside of her thighs.

Her stomach rumbled.

Eric glanced up. His hair mussed, his own body slightly sweaty, his gaze burning with green intensity.

"Hungry?" he asked.

"Always."

"Mmmm." He continued his kissing path upward.

"I also want real food."

His chest rumbled as he chuckled and rolled off her.

The bed they'd claimed for the continuation of their sex-capades lay in disarray—the sheets rumpled and untucked. The room smelled of wood panelling and wool blankets.

"I also need a shower," she said.

"I don't think a loofa will cure that dirty mind."

She smacked his shoulder. "I'm serious."

"So am I." He winked.

She stretched her arms over her head and extended her legs. Her muscles a dichotomy of limber and stiff. Her body, deeply satiated and relieved of months and months of sexual tension, now grew stiff from their rather rigorous schedule and ambitious positions.

"Okay, until the power comes back, an actual shower is out," Eric said. "But there should be enough water in the tank to fill a bowl and we have some bottled water. I could arrange sponge baths for our mutual satisfaction. Then we could delve into a hearty breakfast."

"Lunch."

He peered out the window and squinted. "Lunch."

She waited for Maisie to perk up. That wolf loved everything food related. The werewolf remained quiet. The few times Brenna had reached out, Maisie gently pushed her away, sighing in content bliss. Wow. Her wolf's lust must really be sated if not even food elicited a response.

Brenna's stomach rumbled at the promise of food. "Independent sponge baths first. Then food. I have a feeling your idea of bathing will lead to something else."

"See?" He ran a finger down her bare arm. "Dirty mind."

She snorted, pushed his arm away and sauntered off to find what she needed for a sponge bath. Without power, the hope of an actual shower was out, but she could heat some water, find a cloth and make do. After she finished, Eric took a turn.

After their "baths," they returned to the bedroom to change. Brenna's clothes from the previous night still hung in front of the fire, crusted with dried hot chocolate. So she went on a hunt for spare clothing. With an easy silence, Brenna climbed into a dark maroon velvet dress with a lace back and hem. She'd found it in a closet and smiled as memories poured through her mind. She'd forgotten it here ages ago for a rare appearance at one of her parents' New Year's Eve parties, but thankfully it still fit. Anything was better than wearing the snow, dirt, and hot chocolate encrusted clothing from yesterday.

Eric slipped a pair of sweatpants over his ass. His previously borrowed clothes lay in tatters after he had to shift into a werewolf, but he discovered more clothing stashed in one of the dressers upstairs. Shifters stashed clothes everywhere they could. He lifted the shirt he found from the bed and his gaze flicked to her.

She shook her head. Why bother with the shirt when she'd just rip it off him later?

His grin widened, and he left the shirt on the bed. His muscles rippled, and she drank in the sight of his well-toned body. That V killed her.

A memory of tracing it with her tongue streaked through her mind. Mmmm.

"Come on." Eric grabbed her hand and led her to the kitchen. He made instant coffee by boiling water in a pot over the fire while Brenna made sandwiches.

Luckily, most of the stuff she'd brought didn't go bad in one day, and the ham had been left in the cold storage room.

With hunger pains stabbing her stomach, Brenna shoved the food in her mouth. Her lip split when she tried to get more food in. With a wince, she flicked her gaze to Eric. He hadn't noticed any of her table manners, or lack thereof—too busy stuffing food into his own face with the same frantic vigour. She laughed, and Eric paused with half a sandwich shoved in his mouth to glance at her.

"I still don't see why we had to get dressed for this," Eric muttered with a mouth full of food. He paused, glanced down at his bare chest, and sent her a wink. "Well, mostly dressed."

"I don't want our bare asses on the furniture."

He raised a dark eyebrow.

"Well, okay. Not *all* the furniture." She grabbed a quick swig of water. "If we did, I'd have to admit the possibility my brother and his harem of harlots have done the same thing, and that's just icky."

"Harem of harlots?"

"He's a bit of a player," she said.

"He's not playing them if they're aware of the situation and agree to it."

She nodded, but her thoughts kept running laps inside her head. They hadn't had any serious conversations, at least none in the English language. They hadn't spoken about tomorrow, or after the cabin, or what, exactly, they were doing. Was this a situation? Was she "aware" of it, and by lack of denial, agreeing to it?

She sensed their stolen moments meant as much to Eric as they did to her, but maybe she sensed wrong. Maybe that was hopeful conjecture. Maybe they were on different pages, or hell, reading entirely different books. Maybe this was only a physical thing for him, another wondrous notch in his belt as he told lies with his body.

She shook the thought away. She refused to ruin this weekend with her self-doubt. She'd already made a deal with herself to save all serious conversations for after the blizzard. That way she could escape any awkwardness caused by a second spurning. And really, could any rejection be harder to handle than the one he'd already made?

Eric repeated "harem of harlots" under his breath

again and shook his head. He polished off the rest of the food.

She pulled dessert from her pocket and placed it on the table beside Eric's plate.

"What's this?" he asked.

"Candy hearts. They're a Jones tradition. I brought a bunch of packages to binge on during my read-athon."

Wow did her plans for this weekend change.

"I love these things." He snatched the package from the table's smooth surface. After ripping it open, he pulled out the candies, one by one, reading their messages before placing them in a pile.

"What are you doing?" she asked. "That's not how you eat them!"

She reached out to grab the candy, but he batted her hand away playfully.

"Relax. There's more than one way to eat something." He waggled his brows at her.

"Pig."

"Not what you called me last night."

She bit her lip. "Seriously, though. That's not—"

"Shhh."

He continued the practice until he pulled out a pink heart, no different than any of the previous pink hearts he'd placed in the pile and smiled.

"Aha!" He held it up and glanced at her. His brows pinched together, and his mouth compressed into a thin line before he turned to her. His expression soft-ened but remained serious.

"It's just candy," she said.

"Not to me," he replied. "I want you to have this."

He held out his hand, palm open. She plucked the candy and flipped it around in her fingers.

BE MINE stared back at her.

Something expanded in her chest. Something warm and delicious. She glanced up to find Eric smil-ing, hesitantly, as if unsure of her response.

"I know I can't undo time or past mistakes, but I want to build something new. With you. I want you to be mine."

Brenna's mind blanked. What seemed like hours, probably lasted mere seconds, but her mind reeled at Eric's direct statement. Sure, they'd spent the night phys-ically enjoying one another, but did she want more from him? Still? After all these years and the pain he caused?

Yes. She did. He'd proven himself to be a different man, a better man. It took every ounce of self-control not to leap across the space separating them, knock him out of the chair and plaster her body onto his.

She bit her lip again and stared down at the offered candy. Would she be his? "I think I am already."

Eric surged forward and grasped her head between both large hands. His mouth found hers. His tongue plunged in. The force of his kiss almost knocked her off the chair, but he scooped her up and gently lowered her to the hard floor instead. The chair tipped back and clattered against the floor beside them.

Her wolf howled in her mind.

In seconds, he had her undressed and splayed out as he thrust into her. Every nerve ending hummed with pleasure, with the feeling of how *right* this moment was.

CHAPTER 14

E ric walked down the stairs with weightless shoulders and a spring in his step. As the storm outside abated during their second night together, Eric and Brenna worked through his wish list—or at least made a heroic effort. It was, after all, a long and ambitious list.

Between sharing their dreams and cuddling while they slept, entangled in each other's limbs, they made love—almost as if a sense of urgency drove them to get everything out of this weekend, almost desperate and frenzied, as if they both feared leaving the cabin would dispel some or all of the magic they'd created inside.

Well, he refused to let that happen. Despite promising to wait until the storm blew over for any serious conversations, he'd initiated *the* conversation, with candy of all things. *Smooth, Buchanan.* His lack of refinement didn't matter, though. Not to him, and from all appearances, not to Brenna, either. His heart was in. His wolf was in. He was all in.

It didn't matter that she'd spurned him ten years ago. He'd hurt and humiliated her, and he deserved it. They might never have a true mate bond, or the mating frenzy that went along with the ritual where they pledged themselves to each other under the full moon, but they could still have something special.

After killing the feral werewolf, he'd almost fallen into an irretrievable rage himself. The feral had been so close to hurting Brenna and he'd lost it. He tracked down the other werewolf and ripped him to shreds, almost losing his humanity in the process. He'd returned to the cabin a complete mess, unable to regain control of his wolf, but the moment he sensed Brenna, the moment he smelled her, the second he saw her, it was as if a dark cloud looming over him disappeared. Only Brenna's presence had calmed him. He refused to let that go.

He placed his bag next to the door and turned to watch Brenna's hand tremble as she stuffed the last item into her backpack. Time to find out if Brenna truly reciprocated all the things he'd felt, all the things he'd purred as he gave her a *very* thorough sponge bath.

He grinned.

Brenna caught his knowing look. She glanced away, but not before her cheeks flamed that adorable red.

With cell reception back, and the blizzard blown

out, Brenna had called her father to pick her up, and his parents were making their way over as soon as they could dig out their vehicles. Their snowmobiles sat under a few feet of snow, and probably wouldn't start without being plugged in for a few hours. He could shift and run back, but he didn't want to leave Brenna.

You don't want her out of your sight because you're worried she'll change her mind, Brutus said.

He clenched his fists and forced his shoulders down. *Are you complaining?*

Not at all.

He watched Brenna mill around the room. His whole body thrummed from overuse, but he still wanted to wrap her in his arms and curl up with her on the couch.

"Wish we had more time up here," he admitted as he walked up from behind and pulled her in for a hug. He pressed his lips into her neck and inhaled her rosy scent. Her butt pressed into his groin, and his body ached for her. He closed his eyes and enjoyed her warmth.

Ours, Brutus growled.

"Me, too," she sighed, oblivious to his inner wolf's claim. "But I have to get back for my early shift tomorrow."

He nodded and squeezed her tight. "I'm lucky to have tomorrow off. I'll try to get your truck up and running, but if that fails, I'll arrange for a tow."

She pulled out of his grasp and picked up the

remaining bags. He moved her backpack beside the door.

They'd already cleaned up the living room, bedroom, kitchen, and bathroom. There wasn't anything left to do but wait.

Wait for the end?

Fuck that. He told her he wanted a relationship, and he'd meant it.

Why did she look so nervous then? Why did her hands tremble? Did she doubt him? She shouldn't. He lived in Vancouver, the same city and only a thirty-minute commute away from her place. They'd make this work.

"Brenna." Her name rolled off his tongue.

She stopped visually sweeping the room and turned to him. "Yes?"

"I—"

Bam!

The cabin's front door slammed open and interrupted what he'd planned to say.

CHAPTER 15

Brenna stood in shock as a blonde bombshell with a classic hourglass figure, big ski-bunny hair, and a porn-star worthy pout barged into the cabin and threw her considerable charms all over Eric. Her body wrapped around his, like an octopus attacking prey, and her strong werewolf scent bopped Brenna on the nose.

"Eric!" she squealed. "I was so worried."

Eric's parents clambered into the cabin through the open door and wiped their feet on the rug. Paul Buchanan looked like an older replica of Eric, with the same powerful, tall build and sandy hair. He radiated control and power. Brenna forced her wobbly knees to remain straight instead of cowing under his alpha gaze. She wasn't in his pack she didn't have to submit to him.

Shannon Buchanan, on the other hand, held little

resemblance to her son, save her piercing green gaze. Eric's mom stood beside her husband, tall and regal.

Still extremely aware of the mewling blonde fawning over the man she'd practically licked from head to toe hours ago, Brenna squeezed her fists tight and turned to Mr. and Mrs. Buchanan.

"Hello," Brenna said. "It's been a long time."

Eric's parents nodded, his father with a slight frown and turned down mouth, and his mother with a semi-distracted smile. A null werewolf was of little importance. They barely glanced her way before returning their attention to the spectacle behind Brenna.

Whatever Eric's parents saw pleased them, because their eyes twinkled, and they exchanged satisfied smiles.

"Who's that?" Brenna nodded her head at the blonde. There had to be a reasonable explanation for this.

"The future Mrs. Eric Buchanan," Eric's mom gushed. "A perfect fit for an alpha's mate."

Maisie howled. *No!*

Fire raced through Brenna's veins, and her face heated. The urge to challenge the other woman rose, but she swallowed it down. She was no match for a true werewolf. She didn't have that aggressive chip on her shoulder. If Eric wanted this woman instead, that was his choice. She took a deep breath and turned to find the blonde still draped over Eric, petting his hair and face while mumbling incoherently. Brenna recognized her now. Heather Dufaine, the daughter of the Sapphire pack. With her and Eric mated, the two packs would merge and form a giant, powerhouse. No wonder Mr. and Mrs. Buchanan looked so pleased.

Eric sent Brenna a panicked look over the blonde's shoulder, then tried to untangle himself.

Too late. He could've thrown the woman aside had he wished to. He could've fought for her.

Brenna bit back a sob. She looked around desperately. For what? An escape hatch? A wormhole to swallow her?

Maisie growled. *Our mate.*

No, girl. He hasn't been our mate for a long time and now he never will be.

Another truck pulled up outside, crunching the snow as it turned around.

Her father. Thank God. He always had impeccable timing. "That's my dad," Brenna explained. Eric's parents were too busy watching their son and future daughter-in-law to care.

Brenna surged forward and grabbed her bag.

Un-fucking-believable.

She fell for his charm and lies, again, but this time she gave him more than a heated kiss during a stolen moment. She'd given her body and heart. He wasn't supposed to be capable of hurting her more than he already had. How wrong she'd been.

Be mine, he'd asked, while handing her that silly candy heart.

Mentally face-palming, cheeks aflame, she made a hasty goodbye to Eric's parents and withdrew quickly from the room. She hustled through the deep snow to her dad's waiting truck.

"Brenna! Wait!" Eric's voice called out from behind her.

She ignored him and threw her bag into the back of her dad's truck, wrenched the passenger side door open and dove into the seat.

Her dad beamed at her. "Hey pumpk—"

"Drive!" she barked.

Her dad snapped straight. His wrinkled forehead bunched as he frowned, but thankfully he didn't question her. He shoved the truck into gear, pressed the gas pedal, and drove away.

"Brenna!" Eric's voice called out again as the truck turned the corner and travelled farther from the cabin.

She slipped down in her seat and crossed her arms. To hell with Eric. She should never had fallen for the lies from his clever tongue.

Her dad slowed the truck after a few bends in the road. They passed her truck still embedded in the snowbank. Her dad's mouth turned down at the corners. The damage to the truck looked worse in the daylight. Nothing appeared salvageable. Poor Old Blue. When she called Dad, he'd been upset about the vehicle, but infinitely more relieved she was okay, and the "large scrap of metal" protected her. Looking at Old Blue now, she'd been lucky to survive the crash with insignificant injuries.

Without a word, they rolled past the wreckage.

After a couple silent, and tense, kilometers, and more than a few sideway glances from Dad, he finally spoke up. "Pumpkin, are you okay?"

She sighed and dropped her head back on the seat. "Better now. Thanks for picking me up. Sorry about Old Blue." *Sorry about this whole weekend.*

What was the saying? Fool me once, shame on you. Fool me twice... Well, Brenna was probably a fool during this entire situation. It didn't make the cut any less deep, nor the sting less dull.

Maisie whined.

Her dad nodded, thumbs tapping the steering wheel.

"Did something happen at the cabin?"

Her face flamed as images stroked her memory, ones filled with Eric's naked body pressed to hers, the slow pumping of his hips, the rhythmic movement of their entangled bodies, the heated kisses, Eric's tongue, Eric's fingers, Eric's green gaze, his heart beating hard against her chest...

Goddammit!

She squeezed her eyes shut. "Nothing happened."

"Does 'nothing' have anything to do with Eric Buchanan chasing after us barefoot in the snow hollering your name?"

"Maybe."

Her dad nodded again. His knowing face crinkled with age and laugh lines. "You know, that young man makes a point to ask about you whenever we run into him. Always figured he carried a little torch for you."

"Maybe."

Her dad's hands tightened on the steering wheel, and hard plastic squeaked from the pressure. The truck slowed down as if he prepared to turn around. A low growl rumbled from his chest and his eyes flashed yellow. "He didn't hurt you, did he?"

"No, Dad. He didn't hurt me." Not physically, anyway. Not in the way her father feared. Emotionally...well, emotionally, she was a mess.

She straightened in her seat. She'd gotten over him once. She could do it again.

"Then what's..." her dad started.

"The problem?" she interrupted. "He's engaged."

Her dad's mouth dropped open to form a perfect "O" and silence filled the cab of the truck for the rest of the drive.

One thing she loved about Dad, among many things, was he never minced words, never tried to paint a bad reality with rainbows and daffodils, nor tried to give her clichéd lines as a bandage solution. No expressions of fish in the sea or being better off. He remained quiet because he must've known nothing he could say would solve the ache in her heart.

CHAPTER 16

Eric stomped back into the cabin and slammed the door. The whole cabin shook. He turned to his parents, the wolf pressing hard against the inside of his skin. His gums stung as his werewolf teeth pushed for release. "What the hell was that?"

Mom and Dad jerked back, while Heather frowned.

"What do you mean?" Mom said.

"You told Brenna Heather was going to be my wife." He bit the words out, struggling to maintain control. His canines elongated and blood trickled onto his tongue.

Brutus howled and scratched at his bones. *Let me out.*

No way could he let his wolf out now, the beast would rage and wouldn't care who he hurt.

"And what's wrong with that?" Mom's mouth

turned down. "And why would it matter what I said or didn't say to that girl?"

"She's a null," Dad added.

"She's my mate."

Mom gasped. Dad turned away. Silence descended in the cabin. The stillness of the snow-covered mountain surrounded them.

Heather covered her mouth with her hand, eyes wide. Pain briefly flickered across her expression. "Your mate?"

He nodded.

She squeezed her eyes shut, tensed for a moment, before her entire posture relaxed. "A true mate?" She shook her head. "I never had a chance."

He didn't know what to say to that, so he remained silent.

Heather frowned and glanced back at the door. "Why are you here with us? Go after her."

He took a deep breath, thankful Heather had the decency to understand when his parents couldn't string two words together. "I tried. She left."

"I...I don't understand," Mom said. "You've known Brenna for ages. You practically grew up together. You're friends with her brother. How did you not know earlier?"

Dad studied him, expression grim. "You knew."

Eric sighed and turned away, the silent accusation clear in his father's tone. "I've known since I was eighteen. I...I hurt her, and she left."

"Why would you do such a thing?" Heather asked. "A true mate is a gift."

"I was young, and dumb. I wasn't expecting to find a true mate, especially not so soon after turning eighteen."

"Did you not like her?" Heather asked.

Eric barked out a laugh, more bitter and jaded. "I loved everything about her. Still do."

"Then...why?" Heather scratched her head. "I don't understand."

"I worried what it would mean to have Brenna as my mate," he said. "Especially when I'm going to take over the pack one day."

"Because she's a null?" Mom asked, voice smoother and calmer.

He nodded.

"But...nulls are to be cherished," Heather sputtered.

They all turned to her.

"Nulls are crucial to maintaining a stable pack. They help balance the energy. We have three in our pack and we'd be lost without them. When the young wolves struggle for control, we have them paired off with our nulls so they can feed the calming vibes and master their dominance over their inner wolves." Heather shrugged. "I thought all packs knew that."

Eric groaned. His didn't and he was pretty sure Brenna's pack didn't either. After he'd tracked the feral wolf down in the forest, part of him got lost in the kill.

When he returned to the cabin, his wolf had been in control and Eric liked it. He liked the power and the simplicity. He'd stood at the precipice of sanity, almost losing himself to the rage. The moment he caught Brenna's scent, though, the rage abated. If he'd been standing on a cliff, teetering toward falling over, she pushed him away from danger. It all made sense now.

Dad looked like he wanted to break something, not out of anger, but frustration. "We didn't know. I didn't know."

"You...you need to make this right," Heather said.

"I intend to." He'd let Brenna walk out of his life before, but he wouldn't make that mistake again. He pulled off his sweater and shirt and ignored his parent's matching frowns. "I need to run first."

Brutus howled, impatient to run free. He needed to make things right and that couldn't involve snarling. After he calmed down, he'd make a plan.

CHAPTER 17

Eric's stiff suit chafed, and his gaze kept darting to the clock on the wall. His tight collar dug into his throat, and he itched to tear off his tie and run out of the office. The courier in front of him shifted his weight, back and forth, on the other side of Eric's desk. His face bunched up in displeasure, and his hair stuck to his forehead. At the end of the workday, he probably hated getting called for a last-minute job. He looked ready to drop, but Eric had already promised him extra for this special delivery.

Eric's hands fumbled to tie the small bow.

Once again, he cursed his parents. Not the first time their scheming and tunnel vision had pissed him off, and probably not the last, but in this particular instance, they might've cost him something far more significant than his momentary pride.

Brenna had ignored his calls and texts all week.

Probably deleted his voicemails without listening to them, too.

Being an alpha werewolf didn't excuse him from the mundane responsibilities of life. Money didn't magically appear because of his inherent awesomeness and if he ran off to take care of werewolf business all the time, he'd lose his job. He needed to work to earn a paycheque like everyone else. Work had been hectic and inescapable this week, but thoughts on how to make things right plagued his mind.

He hadn't really done anything wrong. Not during this decade, anyway. Even a herculean effort couldn't unlatch the perversely strong clutches of Heather Dufaine. And as the daughter of the alpha from an allied pack, he couldn't just toss her to the side. Heather might not be the wolf for him, but she deserved his respect.

If his parents had kept their projected desires to themselves, or Brenna hadn't jumped to conclusions and sprinted off like an Olympian runner, he could've sorted the situation out, then and there. But no. Fate liked to knee him in the balls any chance it got.

When he'd shuffled back to the cabin after his run in wolf form, he'd found the gears of calculation already turning behind his mother's green gaze. His dad had moved past the disappointment, anger and frustration, expression turning thoughtful. They prob- ably already envisioned joint-family excursions to the cabins during the summer and winter holidays surrounded by a horde of grandchildren.

He needed to win Brenna back first.

After everything they'd said and done, after everything they'd shared, she'd taken off, assuming the worst, and refusing to give him an opportunity to explain. How could she not know that weekend meant more than a casual hook-up?

The courier cleared his throat. Eric ignored him and continued wrapping the special package.

Eric knew how it looked to Brenna. He knew she doubted all of it. Again.

"You about done, man?" the young courier asked. "Rush hour is going to hit."

Brutus snarled.

The tone scraped against Eric's nerves, too, but he shrugged it off. He sealed the small parcel and handed it to the courier. The brown packing paper made it look even smaller in his hands. Would his present be enough?

Would his plan work?

His heart pumped rapidly in his chest as the courier snatched the package roughly from Eric's hands and slapped a sticker on it. After scanning the box, the courier chucked it in his bag.

Eric's shoulders tensed, and he clenched his jaw.

His heart was in that little box.

The courier held the scanning device out for Eric

to sign without a word. His impatience to get away evident in his tense muscles.

Eric quickly signed his name and handed the courier a tip. The long hand of the clock hit the twelve and signaled the end of the workday, along with Eric's torturous waiting.

"Thanks," the courier muttered before swiveling around and stalking out of the office.

Eric grabbed his stuff and followed.

"Eric?" Lynette from accounting caught up to him as he made his way to the elevator, where the courier already stood waiting.

"Yeah?" He pressed the down button. The courier glowered at him, but when he shifted to take in Lynette, he straightened and smiled.

Lynette spared the courier a tight smile before turning to Eric. "We're going out for drinks. Did you want to join us?"

The elevator doors dinged open, and Eric followed the courier inside without hesitation. He turned to face Lynette. With long, lush brown hair, falling in soft curls, a long sinewy body made more for the runway than crunching numbers, he'd once considered getting to know Lynette better. But she wasn't a wolf and lacked something he wanted. She wasn't Brenna.

Now, she was simply a pretty girl he worked with.

"Sorry, Lynette," he said. "I have to be somewhere."

Her pout showed her disappointment before the doors closed.

"Dude!" the courier whispered. "Big mistake."

Eric grinned and shook his head. "Not at all."

The courier shrugged and readjusted his bag's strap.

Big mistake? His only mistake had been letting Brenna go ten years ago. He didn't plan to make that mistake again.

CHAPTER 18

Brenna had made a huge mistake! Colossal. As she pulled her brown leather riding boots over her black skinny jeans, she replayed Eric's messages on her answering machine. At first, she'd kept them to stay angry. Then she'd kept them to hear the deep tenor of his voice. Then she kept them to ease the pain in her heart and calm Maisie who practically howled continuously since she fled the cabin.

The last words of his message knocked the wind out of her. "I know you already rejected me as a mate all those years ago, but I want a second chance. Or a third. I want to make this right."

He thought she rejected him? The implications of those words made her head spin. She'd never willingly abandon him or the true mate bond. And if he truly thought she had, that meant he'd never officially rejected her.

Told you, Masie huffed. *Mate.*

Her heart pounded heavy in her chest as her imagination ran wild with her understanding of the mating frenzy, replacing the main characters from the stories with her and Eric. She swallowed and tried to get her hands to stop shaking. She could have him. He was still hers...unless she messed everything up.

She listened to his messages again, followed by the one his parents had left unbeknownst to their son. Then the one from her own dad, who'd apparently talked to the Buchanans as well.

Then, finally, the last message, and undoubtedly the most shocking of all the messages.

The message from Heather Dufaine: *"I want a man to speak about me the way Eric talked about you. There was never anything between us, besides our parents' wishes, and maybe a few of mine as well. We never had a chance. I never had a chance. And I want you to know that. I wish you all the best."*

Brenna's stomach lurched, and her heart ached in her chest. She squeezed her eyes shut for a moment before opening the hall closet.

The woman probably got her number from Eric's parents or her own, but her message split Brenna's emotions in half. Knowing Eric spoke of her warmed Brenna's heart, and having Heather care enough to clarify the situation sent a wave of gratitude through her heart. But she also regretted all the dumb blonde thoughts and unjustly cursing the walking pinup.

Brenna had assumed the worst of Eric and took off without giving him the opportunity to explain, without letting everything they'd shared that weekend speak more than one parental comment—one easily misinterpreted, apparently.

She grabbed her jacket from the hanger and pulled it on over her flowing shirt. With Eric's address stored in her phone, she had plans to execute.

After spending half this week unbelievably angry at him, Eric's calls and texts had stopped. Then she'd learned the truth. Fear had struck Brenna's fingers numb and incapable of dialing the phone, and she spent the remaining half of the week racked with guilt and shame.

She had to make things right.

But as the work week finished, no ideas or magical solutions came to her. So Brenna pulled her big girl socks up and decided to go to Eric's place. She'd be direct and apologize.

With a bottle of wine.

And hopefully her naked body slapped against his.

She flicked the lights off. As she reached to open the door, someone knocked. Her heart bolted into her throat. Her hand froze inches from the door handle.

Eric?

She leaned forward and peered through the peephole.

Her stomach sank.

Not Eric.

Some young courier. He swayed a bit on the other side of the door and looked ready to collapse.

A long breath escaped her lungs. Her shoulders dropped. Better see what the courier had for her. Maybe he had the romance novels she ordered last week online.

Or maybe a bill. She turned the knob and swung the door open. A waft of sweat and the cool night air hit her.

She smiled and said, "Hello."

The courier rocked back on his heels. His eyes widened, and his mouth parted.

After it appeared the courier planned to remain speechless, Brenna took a step outside. "Do you have something for me?"

He'd better make this fast. She had places to go. Apologies to make. History to correct. Wolves to mate.

"Yeah, sorry." The courier shook his head and seemed to collect himself. "Just made sense of something a customer said."

She waited. Her toes itched to tap, but she clenched her teeth and folded her arms over her chest.

Maisie whined.

The courier dug out a small package from his delivery bag and held it out to her. She unfolded her arms and plucked the light parcel from his open palm. Before she could really look at it, the courier jutted his other hand out with a large gray handheld device.

"Please sign," he said.

She plucked the little pointer thingy from his hand, and electronically signed her name. Her gaze kept darting back to the package. A courier sticker covered her name and address, but the sender information stared back at her with bold black lettering. From Eric Buchanan.

Her heart stopped.

"Thank you," the courier said. "Have a great night."

"Yeah," she mumbled. "You, too."

Eric sent her something?

She ripped open the bland brown packing paper, meticulously wrapped over a small pink box with a white bow. She'd pick up the paper later. As she stood in her doorway, she untied the bow and opened the box.

The sugary sweet smell of candy rose to her face.

Her eyes stung. Watery vision took in the small heart-shaped pieces. She plucked one out and flipped it over.

BE MINE, it read.

She popped it in her mouth, and the sweet flavour spread to coat her tongue.

She picked up another candy heart and read it.

BE MINE.

She gasped and dropped the candy back in the box, rifling for another one.

BE MINE.

And another.

BE MINE.

She continued to sort through the small box. They all said the same thing. How many packages had he gone through to make this?

Warmth spread through her chest, ballooning and intensifying with each candy she looked at. A white card lay on the bottom. She pulled it out. Little specs of coloured sugar encrusted its surface and decorated Eric's even writing.

I meant every word, he wrote. *My heart is yours.*

Her own heart beat heavy and fast, punching against her ribs and making her vision waver. She clutched the box to her breast and blinked back tears threatening to spill from her stinging eyes.

"Do you have any idea how many packages of candy I had to go through?" Eric said, echoing her earlier thought.

Brenna jumped at the sound. Her head snapped up.

There at the foot of the stairs stood Eric Buchanan.

"I've missed you." His voice, deep and resonating, unexpected but completely welcomed, wove around her in a verbal hug.

With the light fading over the horizon with the setting sun, the last rays of the day cast his green gaze in sparkling shadows. The air's cooling breeze ruffled his thick hair. He stood tense, and silent, in a crisp business suit, waiting for her response.

She gripped his present in one hand, hopped down

the three steps, and leapt into his arms. The tears fell freely. The stress she'd held all week flowed from her veins as she held him tightly. Maisie sighed.

She held onto him, relishing the feel of his arms around her. "I never rejected you."

Eric froze, his hands still on her back. "What?"

"I thought you cast me aside. That's why I left and tried to stay away."

"Never," he whispered, squeezing her tighter. "I was a fool, and a coward. After that stunt I pulled with Anna, I assumed you dropped me the moment you turned eighteen and realized what I did. You left right away, and I felt as though my heart had been ripped out."

She shook her head. They'd both mistaken the pain of separation for the famed agony of a rejected bond.

"If I didn't reject you, and you didn't reject me..." His grip on her tightened. He dropped his forehead against hers, his heart beating so hard she felt it through her shirt. "Will you then?"

"Will I what?"

"Be mine?"

Her lips twitched, recalling how she'd answered him the first time. "I already am."

Thank you for reading *Stormbound*. If you enjoyed the story, I would appreciate you letting others know by leaving a review.

For other enticing stories stories, please visit my website at jcmckenzie.ca

ACKNOWLEDGMENTS

This story was originally a contemporary romance written as a part of a candy hearts series coordinated by my then publisher. Writing a story without any supernatural components, however, never felt quite right, so I'm thankful for the opportunity to revise and republish this story, even if it is a little more "cozy" than I tend to write.

A huge thank you to Cassie Patterson, Amy Stadler and Cheryl Doerr for beta reading this new cozy paranormal version of Eric and Brenna's story, and thank you to Calisa Rose, Charlotte Copper, Karilyn Bentley and Shelly Chalmers for beta reading the original version.

Thank you to Lara Parker for editing this story, not once, but twice, and thank you to Book Nook Nuts for proofreading.

This beautiful cover was created by Gabriela from

BRoseDesignz and as soon as I saw it, I knew it was the one, but thankfully, I wasn't stubborn like Eric when it came to recognizing a good thing.

Thank you to my friends and family and as always, thank you to my wonderful readers. I hope you enjoyed this cozy, second-chance paranormal romance.

ABOUT THE AUTHOR

J. C. McKenzie is a book loving, gumboot-wearing, unapologetic science geek. She predominantly writes urban fantasy and post-apocalyptic dystopian fantasy with strong romantic elements. When she's not spinning tales, she's in the classroom sharing her passion for science and mathematics while secretly warping the young impressionable minds of our future to carry out her evil plans for world domination. She lives in the Pacific Northwest with her family.

Visit her at jcmckenzie.ca

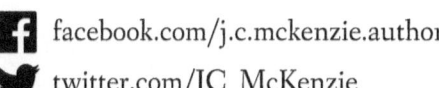

facebook.com/j.c.mckenzie.author

twitter.com/JC_McKenzie

instagram.com/j.c.mckenzie